## "Are we going to address the elephant in the room?"

"Are you talking about this afternoon?" Riley asked.

Wynter nodded.

"I equate it to lust. Pure and simple."

"Do you always speak so plainly?"

"If you mean, am I abason to beat around ... active."

"We grew up ... t me before. Why ...

"You're all grow ... your question, you were always a ... se to me. Even when you were younger, you weren't afraid to have a conversation with me."

"You don't scare me, Riley Davis."

"Perhaps you should be afraid. I bite."

"I don't mind love bites... I didn't mean to say that."

"You don't mean to do a lot of things around me. Do I bring out the best or worst in you, I wonder?"

"That remains to be seen."

\* \* \*

*Her Best Friend's Brother* by Yahrah St. John
is part of the Six Gems series.

Dear Reader,

The idea for this exciting new series came from a girls' trip I took with my besties to Gatlinburg, Tennessee. We used to take these trips annually pre-COVID. While there, I realized it sounded like a good idea for a book. That's how the series Six Gems was born—six girlfriends searching to find Mr. Right while pursuing their dreams.

The first book tells travel blogger Wynter Barrington's story. She, along with the other five gems, inherits a large sum from her aunt, but she has to fight her mother, who wants the money for herself. During this time, she becomes reacquainted with her teenage crush, Riley Davis, who's moved back to San Antonio. Riley is anticommitment because of his mother's mental breakdown after divorcing his father. He's convinced love will only lead to heartbreak, but Wynter sees underneath his icy facade to the man underneath. Can Wynter show Riley true love is worth risking his heart?

Stay up to date with YSJ news by visiting my website or join my newsletter at www.yahrahstjohn.com.

Yours Truly,

*Yahrah St. John*

# YAHRAH ST. JOHN

---

# HER BEST FRIEND'S BROTHER

# HARLEQUIN®
# DESIRE™

Recycling programs
for this product may
not exist in your area.

ISBN-13: 978-1-335-58161-7

Her Best Friend's Brother

Copyright © 2022 by Yahrah Yisrael

For questions and comments about the quality of this book, please contact us at CustomerService@Harlequin.com.

Harlequin Enterprises ULC
22 Adelaide St. West, 41st Floor
Toronto, Ontario M5H 4E3, Canada
www.Harlequin.com

**Printed in U.S.A.**

**Yahrah St. John** became a writer at the age of twelve when she wrote her first novella after secretly reading a Harlequin romance. Throughout her teens, she penned a total of twenty novellas. Her love of the craft continued into adulthood. She's the proud author of forty-two books with Harlequin Desire, Kimani Romance and Arabesque as well as her own indie works.

### Books by Yahrah St. John

### Harlequin Desire

### *The Stewart Heirs*

*At the CEO's Pleasure*
*His Marriage Demand*
*Red Carpet Redemption*

### *Locketts of Tuxedo Park*

*Consequences of Passion*
*Blind Date with the Spare Heir*
*Holiday Playbook*
*A Game Between Friends*

### *Texas Cattleman's Club*

*Vacation Crush*

### *Six Gems*

*Her Best Friend's Brother*

Visit her Author Profile page at Harlequin.com, or yahrahstjohn.com, for more titles.

You can also find Yahrah St. John on Facebook, along with other Harlequin Desire authors, at Facebook.com/harlequindesireauthors!

To my best friends: Therolyn Rodgers,
Tiffany Griffin, Tonya Conway
and Mattie Alexander.

# One

"Hello?" Wynter Barrington called out as she used her key to enter her family's estate in Terrell Hills, located northeast of downtown San Antonio. She plopped her large duffel bag and suitcase on the floor, tossed her keys in the antique bowl on the table and shook off her jean jacket. It was early January, and she'd forgotten how cold it could get in Texas. Today it was forty degrees. When she'd made it to baggage claim, Wynter had hoped a family member would be there to pick her up, maybe with a thicker coat? Instead, there had been no one.

*Was she surprised?*

Her father, Gregory Barrington, was always caught up with work and building his wealth, as if there weren't enough zeros in his bank account. Her mother, Melinda, flitted about from one charity or social meeting to another. And her older brother, Corey? Ever since they were kids, he'd seemed intent on antagonizing her. He would push her down in the mud and dirty her school uniform or dunk her in the pool. It was no wonder she had decided to forgo Christmas with the family in favor of another month in Bali.

Wynter took in the freshly polished black-and-white marble floors, the gorgeous spiral chandelier, the long, sweeping staircase to the second floor and the stone-covered arches to the main rooms. An enormous bouquet of calla lilies stood center stage on the foyer table. Everything looked the same, but it didn't feel the same.

She couldn't believe she was here for her aunt Helaine Smith's funeral. Helaine had passed away in her sleep a few days ago from a brain aneurysm. Her aunt had been the one person in the family who stood by Wynter's side, even if she didn't agree with Wynter's actions. A year ago, Wynter was so unhappy that she chucked her job at the family's investment empire, where she'd been working in the marketing department, and escaped her ho-hum life. Why? Because she wanted to be like her aunt, who'd led a bohemian lifestyle and traveled the globe.

Her family thought Wynter was off her rocker, but Helaine had always been supportive. Wynter was determined to make her travel and leisure blog, *Wynter's Corner*, a success. It didn't just focus on travel content, but instead was about immersing oneself in another culture and trying new foods or activities off the beaten path. She gave tips and tricks on finding cheap flights and accommodations and creating fun-filled itineraries, all the while keeping money in your wallet, but the blog wasn't always lucrative. Subsequently, she'd been receiving a monthly stipend from her father to cover some of her expenses.

For most of her life, she'd felt invisible to the Barrington clan, which was why she'd acted out in her youth to get their action, but that attitude always managed to land her in hot water. Meanwhile, Corey was living up to their father's dreams. He was a workaholic, just like the elder Barrington. Then there was Francesca, Corey's pretentious wife. Wynter wasn't a fan, because Francesca looked down at Wynter when *she* came from a working-class family.

Life as a Barrington was an endless merry-go-round of staying on top and trying to stay relevant. It was why Wynter had left home the first opportunity she could.

She was heading to her room when Agnes, their longtime housekeeper, rushed toward her and enveloped Wynter in a warm hug. Now *this* she remembered, Wynter thought as the Spanish woman held her tight. Agnes had been with their family since she was a child. Agnes was the one who had told Wynter about the birds and bees. Her mother had been too busy to explain what was happening to Wynter's body as she had navigated puberty.

Agnes grabbed both sides of Wynter's face with her weathered palms. "I'm so sorry to hear about Miss Helaine. She was such a good woman."

Wynter nodded. "Thank you, Agnes. She was phenomenal."

"We need more like her." Agnes touched her cheek. "How are you doing?"

"I'm coping," Wynter responded honestly.

"That's all you can do, but if you want to talk…"
Agnes left the statement open-ended. Wynter appreciated that Agnes didn't push. Instead, she asked, "How
about you go wash up and get ready? Dinner will be
here before you know it, and you know how your mother
is."

Boy, did she, Wynter thought.

Her mother required everyone to dress for dinner as
if it was a formal occasion. Wynter hated it. She had
always felt less than, as though she never measured
up, probably because she didn't. Her mother always
found fault with what she was wearing, her hair or her
makeup. Wynter just couldn't win.

"Sounds like a good idea," Wynter stated and went
to lift one of her bags, but Agnes shooed her away. "I'll
take care of them."

They climbed the spiral staircase to the second floor
and toward Wynter's room, located in the east wing of
the house.

"How long are you staying this time?"

Wynter shrugged. "Not long. Once the funeral is
over, I'll be leaving."

"That's a shame. I would love to have you home for
a while."

"I'm sorry, it can't be helped. Where's my mother?"
Wynter inquired, raising a brow.

"She's having a facial in the spa room downstairs."

"Spa room?"

Agnes chuckled. "Your mother's made some changes
since you were last here. With you gone and Corey married, she said it was time for her."

"I see," Wynter said, but she really didn't. Her mother

always made time to ensure she looked 100 percent perfect before she walked out the door. Heaven forbid anyone see her not looking her best. Wynter would have to accept that her family was never going to be the cast of *Black-ish*, and the sooner she got over that delusion, the better off she'd be.

"We are so glad to have you join the firm." Brock Jamison, one of the partners of the law firm Jamison and Charles, shook Riley's hand later that morning when the partners met him at their office in downtown San Antonio. "We need someone with your killer instinct on our team."

Riley had been dubbed "the Shark of the East" because he knew how to figure out an opponent's weakness, exploit it and flip the script to ensure his divorce cases went his way. Ever since he graduated from Harvard Law School, Riley had pursued excellence. He'd joined a top law firm in New York right out of Harvard and quickly gained a reputation as a shrewd negotiator.

He'd garnered several high-profile clients and minimized their exposure during their divorces. Once word got out that he intended to relocate, firms across the country had jockeyed for him to join them. All they saw were dollar signs, and that was fine with him. Riley knew what it was like to go without, because he and his sister, Shay, had had everything they could ever wish for—until their parents' divorce took it all away.

"I'm excited to be back home," Riley finally said. He'd met with Brock and his partner, Gina Charles, a couple of months ago when they'd flown to Manhattan, where he'd been based. They'd been eager to hire someone with Riley's talents. He was a closer and always got the job done. Although he had always intended to relocate home, he'd made it a condition that his becoming partner had to be on the table. Gina and Brock agreed, and now that he was accredited in Texas, the firm was Jamison, Charles and Davis.

"If you need anything while you're here—" Gina lightly touched his arm on her way out "—just let us know."

He saw the appreciative glint in her eye. Riley knew he was easy on the eyes, because ever since he was fifteen, women of all ages had tended to congregate around him. Today, he was dressed in a three-piece suit that he knew emphasized his six-foot-three frame. When he went to court, he towered over his opponents, which gave him an advantage. He portrayed power, and he usually got what he wanted, when he wanted and how he wanted it.

After Gina and Brock left, Riley placed his briefcase on the modern glass desk and stalked over to the window to look at the view of San Antonio. It was good to be home. He could check on his mother regularly and periodically give his little sister a little tough love. She was working as a yoga and Pilates instructor at a fitness studio in town. Although she had a loyal fan base, surely there was something else she could be doing?

As if she had ESP, his cell phone rang, and the display read Shay. Riley picked it up. "Hey, sis."

"Hello to you, too, big brother," Shay responded. "You got back in town yesterday and didn't come by and see me."

He sighed. What was it about little sisters that they loved to tease their older brothers? "I'm sorry. I got caught up on a case, and today I've been getting acclimated at the new firm."

"And? How is it?"

"Exactly what I expected," Riley said. He never made a move that wasn't well thought out. Shay was the exact opposite. She led with her heart and not her head, which explained her early divorce at twenty-four. Riley, on the other hand, looked at all the angles before diving in.

"That's good, I guess. Can we meet up for dinner? I would love to see you."

"Absolutely—I'd love that," Riley replied, and he meant it. He missed his sister. They'd grown close after their parents' divorce decimated their mother. It had been hard for Eliza Davis to get out of bed some mornings and take them to school or fix them a meal. Eventually, Riley had learned how to fend for himself and subsequently help his four-years-younger sister, who hadn't understood why Mommy couldn't shake off her depression.

"Great. I'll see you tonight at seven?" Shay asked. "I'll pick you up at your hotel."

"That's not necessary. I can meet you someplace."

"Riley, let me do this for you."

It was hard for Riley not to be in charge in their relationship. He was supposed to take care of her, but his Bentley, which he was having shipped from Manhattan, wasn't arriving until tomorrow. "All right. All right, but you'll have to pick me up from work."

Ending the call, Riley glanced around his new corner

office. He'd finally arrived. Maybe it was time to take his foot off the gas and relax a little. He snorted. As if that were possible—he lived for the game.

Wynter awoke from her nap with a start. Glancing around the room, she had to remember where she was, but when she did, the grief she'd kept inside since Bali came hurtling back to the forefront of her mind. Her aunt Helaine was gone. At least she'd passed away in her sleep and hadn't felt any pain. Wynter wished she could have talked to her one more time. Told her how much she loved her. How much she respected her and how thankful she was to have her in her life—but she couldn't.

Instead, she recalled the special moments they'd shared. Like the first time they went for tea and scones when she was eight years old and they wore fancy dresses, hats and gloves. Or the time her aunt took Wynter to Paris and they rode to the top of the Eiffel Tower. Wynter supposed that was where she got her zest for traveling, because her aunt had included Wynter on her trips. And in her teens, her aunt had always included her group of friends, known as the Six Gems, whenever she could on their outings because, she said, they were the daughters she never had.

Slowly, Wynter moved into an upright position. It was dark out, which meant she'd slept longer than she thought. She normally didn't wear a watch, because she liked to enjoy life without being tethered to a schedule. Reaching for her iPhone, she read the time. It was six o'clock—cocktail hour at the Barrington residence. If she hurried, she could shower, dress and be downstairs in fifteen minutes. While traveling abroad, Wynter had learned not to sweat the small stuff. But here? Her mother expected everyone to be on time for dinner, and Wynter was no exception.

Fifteen minutes later, after throwing on a knee-length sweaterdress and her favorite fringed boots, Wynter rushed down the stairs to the great room. The dress wasn't as chic as her mother would expect, but it would have to do, because her wardrobe was limited with Wynter being on the road most of the year. She'd spritzed her naturally wavy shoulder-length hair with shea moisturizer, arched her eyebrows and added a swipe of lipstick.

When she arrived, her mother and father were bickering. Her brother and his wife were drinking wine, but all conversation ceased when they saw Wynter standing in the doorway. Wynter couldn't miss the disdain in their stare. They were all dressed to impress. Her father and Corey looked as if they'd come straight from work in their business suits. They were both of average height, with medium-brown complexions and the same close-cropped haircut. Her mother wore a fit-and-flare jacquard dress, and Francesca was in a slim-fitting black-and-white sheath.

"Wynter, good heavens, what are you wearing?" Francesca asked. Francesca was everything a woman of Wynter's standing was supposed to be: poised, elegant and refined—or so her mother liked to tell her. Tall, at five foot nine, with a slender figure and long ebony hair in a sophisticated cut, Francesca oozed sophistication and made Wynter look dowdy in comparison.

"I got this dress in Bali during my travels," Wynter

replied as she walked in the room and headed to her parents. She mustn't let their negative opinion bring her down. "Mother," she said, giving her a kiss on each cheek. "Daddy." She leaned over to give him the briefest of hugs.

"Glad you could finally join us, darling," her mother replied. "Agnes told us you arrived earlier and went straight to sleep."

"It was a long flight from Bali."

"Perhaps you shouldn't travel so far," Corey replied with a smirk. "Then you would be a little closer to home."

Wynter ignored the dig, reminding herself this visit would be a short one. Once she buried her aunt and said her goodbyes, she would be on her way. "How are you doing, Mother? Losing Aunt Helaine so sudden…"

Her mother's expression softened. "It was a shock. My big sister was always so big and bold. I never thought anything could take her out."

Tears welled in Wynter's eyes. "I can't believe it, either."

"Well, dry your eyes," her mother said, handing Wynter a handkerchief. "We must carry on. It's what Helaine would want."

So much for commiserating over their shared grief. Wynter had hoped her aunt's death might bring her and her mother closer, but now she wasn't so sure.

"I wonder what her will says," Francesca said aloud.

It was one of the first times Wynter had ever heard Francesca say anything in poor taste. Wynter and her mother both scoffed. Even her brother had the decency to look uneasy at his wife's social faux pas.

Francesca lowered her head. "My apologies, Melinda. I don't know what came over me."

Wynter knew. Francesca hoped Aunt Helaine had left Corey a big inheritance, but their aunt had never warmed to her brother. They'd been like oil and water.

"I, for one, am going to miss the old battle-ax," her father stated.

"Gregory!" her mother admonished.

Her father shrugged and drank some of the dark-colored liquid in his crystal tumbler. "What? You know Helaine never thought I was good enough for you. I came from a working-class background, while the both of you were from the upper crust."

"That's all water under the bridge," her mother responded. "Look where you are now."

"I suppose," her father replied grudgingly.

"I'm going to check on dinner."

When her mother left, Corey wasted no time in going in on Wynter. "What have you been up to the last few months, squirt?"

He loved to tease her about her five-foot-two height. "You would know if you followed my blog," Wynter replied and went over to the bar nestled against the far side of the room. She poured herself a bourbon, something she'd gotten used to drinking after a stint in the Bluegrass State.

"Isn't that a rather strong aperitif?" Francesca asked, quirking her overly arched brow.

"I'm twenty-seven years old. I don't need you or anyone else policing what I drink."

Francesca puffed out a breath. "Well, excuse me."

"You are excused." There was no love lost between

Wynter and her sister-in-law. She'd known Francesca since they were teenagers, and she'd been just as hoity-toity in high school as she was now. Back then, after Wynter wrecked her father's brand-new Porsche, her parents retaliated by taking Wynter out of the private high school and placing her in a public one. They thought they were punishing Wynter, but instead she ended up meeting five incredible women who would become her best friends. Meanwhile, Francesca had gotten worse, because she'd married into the family.

"Don't go getting your panties in a bunch," Corey responded. "Franny was probably worried you could have developed a drinking habit or something. Not many women drink bourbon."

Wynter turned her eyes to Corey. "Well, I do." Corey looked as if he was ready to say something back, but her mother announced that dinner was ready. She was thankful for the interruption, because Corey couldn't even manage cordiality. Wynter followed her mother down the hall to the exquisitely decorated dining room, boasting vintage French furniture, where they'd sit for an elaborate four-course meal.

"I'm glad you're back, Wynter," her father said, once the first course of gazpacho was served. "Because it's high time we talk about you coming back to Barrington Investments."

*Here we go again*, Wynter thought, suppressing an eye roll. She knew her father was not a fan of her leaving, but she'd hoped, in time, that he would accept her decision. Apparently, she was wrong. "I'm very happy doing my travel blog."

"A blog that makes you no money," he responded hotly.

"Yes, it does," Wynter replied. It might not be the amount she wanted, but with more followers, she would secure advertising dollars.

"Not enough," her father replied curtly. "And we will no longer subsidize this hobby."

Wynter's eyes darted up from her soup bowl. "Pardon?"

"You're not hard of hearing," her father responded, and she saw Corey smirk from across the table. "It's long past time for you to come back to the firm and work with me and your brother."

"I can't believe you're doing this now," Wynter said. "You couldn't even wait until after the funeral?"

"Delaying won't change my mind," her father stated.

"Mom?" She turned to her mother for help, but Melinda lowered her head as if she were unearthing jewels in her gazpacho.

"Either you come back to Barrington Investments and the marketing department, or you're cut off financially. This family is no longer going to support you gallivanting across the world."

Wynter supposed she shouldn't be shocked. Her parents had never understood her need for freedom and her passion for exploring new cultures. Wiping her mouth with her napkin, she quietly rose from the table and started for the door.

"Well, aren't you going to answer me?" her father asked.

Wynter swung around to face him. "My leaving should be answer enough. I will not be railroaded or blackmailed into doing things your way, Daddy. I have a vision for my future, and it doesn't include sitting behind a desk, shuffling papers."

Her father was outraged while Corey shot daggers at her. "Wynter, I'm warning you…" Her father thumped his fist on the table, causing it to reverberate.

"And I've received your message, loud and clear," Wynter responded. "Mother—" She glanced in her direction. "My apologies, but I won't be staying for dinner. Good night."

Wynter stalked out of the room. The monthly stipend she counted on to supplement her income was gone, and she was going to have to figure out her next move quickly, because her father had drawn a line in the sand. But then again, so had she. She hadn't used the entire allowance every month. Instead, she'd saved the majority of it so she would have breathing room. Wynter was glad she had, because she was going to need it. She only had one life to live, and no one was going to tell her how to go about it. Somehow, she would figure out a way to support herself without coming back home with her tail tucked between her legs.

She just had to come up with a plan.

# Two

"It's so good to have you back, Riley," Shay said when he met her at their favorite restaurant, a cozy family-owned eatery specializing in Italian food on San Antonio's River Walk. They sat at a small table with a red-checkered tablecloth.

Riley took a good, long look at his baby sister, who wore her hair in long dark locks. She'd always been petite, at five foot four, which was why he'd always felt protective, but she was a grown woman now.

"It's good to be back." It had never been his intention to stay away this long. He was supposed to get a college education at Princeton and obtain his law degree somewhere in Texas. Riley had never imagined he'd get accepted into Harvard Law, but once he was, he'd figured out a way to make it work. The problem was, it left Shay alone to deal with their mother's depressive episodes.

"Mom will be thrilled, too. When I told her you were back, her face lit up like it was Christmas."

"I'm sorry I left you alone to deal with the fallout," Riley replied. When he'd been younger, he'd shielded Shay from the damaging effects of their mother's mental health issues, but once he went to school, she'd been left alone to carry the load. He'd been selfish, wanting to carve out a life for himself away from the manic depression that had consumed so much of his teenage years. When he came home, Riley never knew whether their mother would still be in her pajamas at 3:00 p.m. Or if he might get called away from lacrosse practice because she was having an episode.

"It's okay," Shay said, sipping her wine. "It was your time."

"And what about you?"

"What about me?"

"Dealing with Mom can be a full-time job some days," Riley responded. "It couldn't have been easy for you."

It certainly hadn't been for him. It's why he struggled to form lasting relationships—it's why he didn't believe in love. He'd seen firsthand what loving someone could do to you. His mother had never recovered from losing their father. So Riley refused to acknowledge the emotion.

Shay sighed and put down her glass. "It wasn't. It's one of the reasons why Kevin and I had so many troubles, not to mention we were way too young to get married. Kevin couldn't accept that he didn't come first and that Mama needed me."

"Kevin was a knucklehead anyway," Riley replied. "I never understood what you saw in him. He wasn't going anywhere or doing anything with his life. I'm glad you didn't have any kids with him."

"Not for lack of trying," Shay responded dejectedly.

Riley frowned. This was the first time he was hearing about this, and the strain on his sister's face told him it was real. "What are you talking about?"

"Kevin wanted a baby and I wanted to give him one, but the more we tried, the farther apart we became. Add my devotion to taking care of Mama and you have a recipe for divorce." Shay's voice cracked on the last sentence, and Riley reached across the table and placed his hand over his sister's.

"I'm so sorry, Shay. I wish I had known."

Shay shrugged. "There's nothing you could have done."

"Did you see a doctor?"

Shay shook her head. "We were young and barely making ends meet. We couldn't afford a fertility specialist."

"Then there's still a chance you could be a mother someday if that's what you want," Riley replied. And if it was, he would do everything in his power to ensure his sister achieved her dream. It was the least he could do after leaving her with their mother all these years. Once he'd started making real money, he'd hired a caregiver to help, which finally allowed Shay to focus on herself and get her fitness credentials.

"Oh, my God!" Shay chuckled. "How did we get so

far off topic? My fertility, or lack thereof, is beside the point. It's not like there's some man in my life."

"You mean my little sister doesn't have men beating down the door?" Riley teased. Shay was a beautiful woman, with smooth toffee skin and a killer figure most women would be envious of, because she was a health nut. He supposed it had a lot to do with her seeing their mother's downward spiral and wanting to be the antithesis of her.

Shay smiled at him. "Sadly, no, but I wouldn't have the time anyway. I've been focused on my work and helping others achieve their best self."

"You have to make time for you."

"Ha!" Shay laughed, and Riley realized he was the pot calling the kettle black. "You're one to talk. You're as driven as I am. No—" she shook her head "—you're definitely more."

Riley let out a hearty chuckle. "I won't to try to deny it. You're right."

Although their father had sent child support when they were young, he'd checked out on their family when he left, and his children had been left to pick up the pieces. Riley had been ill-equipped to handle the responsibility he'd been given, and the money their father sent hardly covered the household bills when their mother couldn't work. It was why he was so driven now. He never wanted their family to go without again.

"How about we order?" Shay said. "I'm starved. All I had for lunch was a cauliflower rice bowl with some avocado."

Riley frowned. "Sounds appetizing." He signaled the waiter over, and soon they'd ordered enough food

to feed an army. Riley was happy he could be there for
Shay and his mother again. He was at a point in his life
where he'd achieved what he wanted to professionally. It
didn't mean he didn't keep working hard, because that
was what you had to do to stay on top.

"What's next for you?" Shay asked after they finished their meal and were enjoying dessert and cappuc-
cinos. Thanks to her usually healthy eating preferences,
Shay hadn't minded when he suggested a treat.

Riley shrugged. "Maybe buy a house?"

After they finished dessert, Riley escorted Shay back
to her car and then decided to go for a stroll along the
River Walk because it was close to the penthouse he
had purchased.

As he went, he noticed he'd caught the eye of several women. He was used to drawing attention, but one
woman in particular caught his eye, even though she
stood a few feet away, staring off into the distance. She
had tawny skin and tumbling waves of dark hair that
fell to her shoulders, while her figure, in a snug, fitted
sweaterdress, was petite yet curvy in all the right places.
His heart throbbed when he looked at her. Hell, every
part of him throbbed.

Riley didn't know how this beautiful creature had
landed in his lap, but he wasn't going to look a gift horse
in the mouth. He'd wanted to get his feet wet now that he
was back in town, and his prayers had been answered.
But as he moved closer, Riley realized he knew her.
Had grown up with her.

He'd just lusted after his little sister's best friend—
Wynter Barrington.

* * *

Wynter stood on the edge of the river and wondered what she was going to do. She was on her own in more ways than one. Her family had turned against her, but had they ever really been *with* her? She used to go to her aunt, and Helaine would talk her off the ledge. But now she didn't have her aunt to rely on. Wynter supposed that was why she'd come tonight—to feel closer to her in some way. The River Walk had always been one of her aunt's favorite places to talk.

Wynter thought about her girlfriends, the other members of the Six Gems: Lyric Taylor, Asia Reynolds, Teagan Williams, Shay Davis and Egypt Cox, whom she'd met in public high school. Wynter had seen the other five girls around school and wanted to talk to them, but they'd seemed like a close-knit circle, no outsiders allowed. Until one day, a bigger girl picked on Wynter in gym class. Suddenly, the five girls came to her defense because they didn't like bullies, and a friendship was born.

Boys were always trying to hit on them, and Teagan had decided the group needed a name. Egypt had said they were all priceless and any boy would be lucky to date them. Asia had said they were like the gemstones she used in the jewelry she made. Suddenly, the Six Gems came to be. The name stuck, and they'd been using it ever since.

Wynter's friends would be a godsend and offer their support and a crying shoulder if she needed one, but it was late. She didn't want to call them with her troubles. Could they honestly relate to her crisis? She would probably sound like a poor little rich girl, while the rest of them were working hard and saving to start their own businesses. Egypt was hoping to leave her popular Raleigh food truck and open her own restaurant. Former ballerina Lyric was tired of all the dance moms at the studio where she worked in Memphis and wanted her own place. Meanwhile, Shay was adamant she could become the next fitness guru if she had a retail spot. Up-and-coming Phoenix real estate agent Teagan was working toward launching her own brokerage. And Asia's jewelry was selling like hotcakes online and in Denver, but she wanted a brick-and-mortar store.

They all had a goal, and so did Wynter. Hers was to monetize her travel blog. She sat down on a bench to feel sorry for herself.

"Wynter?"

Hearing her name being called was jarring, considering it was nearly 10:00 p.m. Glancing up, Wynter did a double take as she looked into the gleaming depths of Riley Davis's ebony eyes. He wore a white silk shirt with a few buttons undone and dark trousers that hugged his narrow hips while emphasizing his muscular thighs. A suit jacket hung over his impressive shoulders. At thirty-one—she remembered their exact age difference because she'd crushed on him as a teen—he looked rich, powerful and utterly masculine.

"Riley?"

He smiled, revealing a perfect set of white teeth. "One and the same, but what are you doing out here?" he inquired as he moved closer toward her. "It's late."

Wynter soaked Riley in, from the classic haircut framing his chiseled face, to his broad nose, to his generous mouth, surrounded by a trim black beard. He was a fine specimen of male beauty *and* he smelled amazing.

"I needed some air," Wynter found herself saying.

"Is everything okay?" he asked, sitting beside her.

Wynter glanced down and noticed she was clutching the handkerchief her mother had given her earlier. She shook her head. "No, not really. I'm here in town because my aunt…" Her voice cracked on the last word, and she began crying. "She…she passed away a few days ago, and I'm… I'm here for her funeral."

"Wynter, I'm so sorry," Riley responded, and before she could say another word, he pulled her into his arms.

How did he know that a hug was exactly what she needed? What she craved from her own family but hadn't received? She clung to him probably longer than was appropriate, and Riley let her. It felt so good to be held. Wynter felt comforted and protected even though she hadn't seen Riley in years.

She'd once had a serious infatuation with this man, but he'd never treated her as anything other than Shay's friend. However, for a second, when he had approached her, she'd sensed male appreciation in his eyes. Surely she must have been deceiving herself? Wishing something didn't make it a reality.

Reluctantly, she pulled away and blotted her eyes with her sleeve. "Thank you."

"You're welcome. You must have needed that."

Wynter nodded, glancing at him. "I did. My aunt meant everything to me. She was the one person I could count on, and I guess I assumed that meant she would live forever. I know that must sound foolish."

"No, it's not. Her death must have been a shock."

She nodded. "I had planned to return in a few weeks and spend some time with her, but it's too late." She sniffed. "And now I'll never be able to tell her how much she meant to me."

"She knew you loved her. You have to hold on to that and the precious memories you have of her."

Wynter gave him a sideways glance. She didn't remember this kind and caring side of Riley. It went against the ruthless image Shay told her he'd garnered as a divorce attorney. Wynter was interested in this juxtaposition of traits.

"What?" Riley asked when she stared at him intently.

"You're not who I thought you were."

To her surprise, he stared right back, and they locked gazes. Wynter tried to ignore the fluttering of her pulse, but she couldn't. This was Riley, the boy she'd crushed on in her youth, but now he was *all* man. His scent teased her nostrils and tantalized every one of her senses.

"Neither are you, Wynter Barrington," Riley replied. One of his hands began to play with a tendril of her hair in an absent fashion. "You're all grown-up."

Wynter swallowed, unsure of what to do next. If she was reading his signals right, Riley was interested *in her*. She wished she could act on it, but she wasn't in the right headspace to start something she couldn't—or didn't dare—finish. Riley had a reputation as a ladies' man, and she didn't want to be just another notch on his bedpost, no matter how attractive she might find him.

Blinking, she pulled back, and Riley released the tendril. "When did you get back? I'd heard you were doing great things up north."

At her sudden change of topic, his eyes shuttered,

and Wynter could no longer read what he was thinking. Was it that easy for him to turn his attraction for her on and off? Or had she imagined it because she was in distress and her emotions were all over the place?

"This week," Riley answered.

"Will you be staying long?" Wynter was curious how long she would have this enigmatic man in the same stratosphere as her.

"Indefinitely."

"Really?" Her heart lurched, and she let out a long breath she hadn't realized she'd been holding.

"Yeah, I want to be closer to Shay and my mother, so I've relocated back to San Antonio and joined a law practice."

"Congratulations!" Wynter couldn't resist the wide grin that spread across her features. "I know Shay will be very happy."

"I hope she's not the only one," he quipped.

*Now he was definitely flirting with her.*

"Well, I should go." Wynter rose to her feet, and when she did, so did Riley. She didn't want to get ahead of herself. Riley was a bright light in an otherwise unpleasant evening.

"Of course. Can I walk you to your car?"

"That would be lovely, thank you." They walked in companionable silence for a few blocks until she came to the street where her BMW was parked. "This is me."

"Nice ride."

"Thank you." But the more Wynter thought about it, the more she realized she would have to give it up. She couldn't afford the monthly payments or upkeep on this beast. If her family was divorcing her financially, she would have to be more frugal with her money, and keeping a Beamer was *not* within her means. The car had been her college graduation gift to herself. She'd thought she could afford it working for the family business, but that hadn't worked out too well. She would also have to move out of the family mansion. She could put her few meager belongings in storage. If and when she was home, she could always rent an Airbnb; it wasn't like she stayed home for long anyway.

"I'm sorry to hear about your aunt, but if you need anything—" Riley pulled a business card out of the suit jacket he'd been carrying and handed it to her "—this has my personal cell. Call me anytime."

Wynter looked down at the card embossed with his name. He was giving her personal access to him. That meant something, right? Underneath her lashes, she glanced at Riley and found he was staring intently at her mouth. Wynter felt her body temperature rise, and she feared she might do something stupid, so she said, "I just might do that."

Then she spun around and, unlocking the door as fast as she could, jumped inside. The car roared to life as soon as she turned it on. She didn't dare look at Riley. She couldn't. She was too afraid of what she might see there. Lust. Attraction. Desire. Because she was certain he'd felt the heat between them as much as she had.

If she had given Riley the slightest hint that she was interested, what would have happened? Wynter guessed she would never know.

*Damn.*

Had he really been gone that long? When had Wynter become that fine? From the moment Riley saw her on the River Walk, he was attracted to her. She had an hourglass figure, with a round behind, shapely thighs and, Riley guessed, C-cup breasts. She was h-o-t!

He wanted her.

But, damn, if his timing wasn't off. Wynter had suffered a terrible loss and was grieving. It wasn't the right time to make a move, but that didn't mean he didn't want to. She was beautiful, her skin tawny and bright. Her lips full and juicy. And her eyes were light brown with a darker rim around them—they were eyes he could get lost in for hours. And if tonight had been another time and circumstance, he would have taken her back to his penthouse.

He had a high sex drive, and few women could match his intensity in the bedroom. Could Wynter hold her own? Of all of Shay's friends, she was the one he'd noticed because she'd been unable to hide her schoolgirl crush when he returned home during his infrequent visits. Back then, she'd been much too young for him. He'd been twenty years old and she'd been sixteen. He'd been flattered, but had given her a wide berth.

There had been plenty of college-age girls at his disposal who were down for casual sex. After having to care for his mother during high school, Riley had made up for lost time in college and law school. He knew ladies thought he was a playboy with commitment phobia, and it was true. Marriage wasn't on the menu, but good sex was, and Wynter Barrington fit the bill.

He was certain he'd see her again, and if he had his way, the next time, they'd end the night in his bed.

# Three

Wynter stared out of the window of the Barrington estate several days after she'd returned home to San Antonio. Today was going to be tough—it was the day of her aunt's funeral, and she was giving the eulogy. At first, her mother had been against anyone in the family speaking, but Wynter couldn't bury her aunt without telling everyone what a great person she was.

Inhaling deeply, Wynter grabbed her peacoat and headed downstairs. Her family was waiting in the foyer when she arrived. Her father tsked as if she were late, but, checking her watch, Wynter confirmed that she was right on time. Her mother and Francesca wouldn't be able to find fault with her attire of a black cap-sleeved dress, because they were all wearing black, though Francesca had to be over-the-top with a fanciful hat and veil, as if it were *her* aunt she was mourning.

Without a word, Wynter followed her parents, Corey and Francesca to the limo. When they arrived at the church, the parking lot was overflowing with guests; Wynter could only imagine how many people were inside. People had loved and respected her aunt.

Tears welled in Wynter's eyes when she saw her best friends, Shay, Egypt, Lyric, Asia and Teagan, standing on the sidewalk, waiting for her. Shay lived here, but when had the other ladies flown in? After high school, they'd all gone their separate ways, with Egypt, Lyric, Asia and Teagan leaving San Antonio to chase their dreams, but they'd always kept in touch and tried to take annual trips together. She felt their love, and it was like a balm to her soul.

Wait—was that Riley at Shay's side? He'd come to her aunt's funeral? Wynter nearly stumbled as she exited the limo, but her father caught her and helped her straighten.

The funeral director came toward them. "I'm so sorry for your loss."

Her father shook his hand. "Thank you. Is everything in order?"

"Yes, Mr. Barrington. Exactly as your wife requested. We're still waiting on a few guests, but if you'd come with me, I can seat you in our family room until we're ready to start."

Her family headed inside, but Wynter remained where she stood. She needed her friends at a time like this. And, sure enough, once her parents were no longer in sight, the girls rushed toward Wynter and enveloped her in a group hug.

"We're so sorry, girlfriend." Asia spoke first.

"We loved Auntie Helaine," Lyric stated.

"She will be sorely missed," Shay added.

"Th-thank you," Wynter responded. She could barely speak. Glancing up, her eyes connected with Riley's. He was standing a discreet distance away, giving them their privacy, yet she couldn't ignore his presence. He'd comforted her several nights ago when she was trying to make sense of it all. And now, he was here again. Was he paying his respects? Or was there more?

"We're here for you," Egypt said, interrupting Wynter's inner musings. "We're all staying for a couple of days. Isn't that right?" She glanced in the direction of Teagan, whom they all knew was a notorious worka holic and constantly on the grind trying to build her real estate clientele.

Teagan's eyes narrowed, but she replied, "Of course."

"What can we do?" Shay asked. "Anything, anything at all."

Suddenly, Francesca loudly whispered behind her, "Wynter, it's time."

Wynter glanced at the double doors that led to the church, where she would be saying her goodbyes to her aunt for the last time, and then turned back to her friends. "Riley," she said, looking over her friends' shoulders, "would you mind sitting with me today?"

A warm smile spread across his attractive features, and he said, "It would be my pleasure." He walked toward Wynter and she saw her friends' collective mouths drop as he approached. He held out his hand, and Wynter took it as if he were her lifeline before she went underwater.

Together, they walked into the church.

* * *

Riley watched Wynter move sinuously around the living room at the Barrington estate. It was late afternoon, and only close family and friends had been invited to the Barringtons' for the repast. And the family had put on quite a display, which included a caterer, waiters passing appetizers and a food spread that rivaled that of a wedding.

However, he sensed Wynter was on edge after the heartwarming service for her aunt. He didn't know what had made him call Shay earlier that morning to find out the time of the funeral—he'd just known he *needed* to come. And he was glad he had. Wynter had needed him. Maybe not in the way he wanted her to need him someday, but, nonetheless, she had asked him to sit with her.

During the service, he'd held her cold hand in his, patting it when she tightened her hold after a particularly moving speech by one of her aunt's former suitors. When it had been Wynter's turn to give the eulogy, he whispered encouraging words in her ear before she rose to face the audience. She'd put on a brave front speaking about her late aunt and how she'd influenced not only her life, but her friends' lives. Riley had been touched. He hated that she was experiencing such a profound loss. So he'd determined right then and there to stay close to her side for the remainder of the day. Yes, he wanted a more intimate relationship with Wynter, but right now, she needed a friend.

"What's going on between you and Wynter?" Shay materialized at his side when he went to the buffet in the dining room. Rather than having to make himself a plate, the Barringtons had staff on hand to serve the food. After asking for a little bit of everything, Riley accepted his plate, along with a linen napkin set that he assumed held his utensils, and moved out of the line.

"Are you going to answer me?" Shay asked when, rather than speak, he set his plate on a nearby high-top table and began eating. He'd worked through breakfast, checking on cases and making sure everything was in order, so he was starved. As he ate, he watched his sister become annoyed at his silence. He loved giving her a hard time.

Once he'd taken a few bites, he wiped his mouth with the napkin and said, "There is nothing going on between me and Wynter."

Shay cocked her head and folded her arms across her chest. "Why don't I believe you?"

Riley shrugged and continued eating. "Can't I be there for a friend?"

"You and Wynter have never been friends."

"We've gotten better acquainted." Riley ate a few more bites of food.

"How better acquainted?"

"Get your mind out of the gutter, sis," Riley said, even though his mind had gone exactly there on more than one occasion in the past hour, seeing Wynter in her formfitting black dress.

"Like yours isn't there?" Shay whispered. "I know you, Riley, and you have a reputation for being a ladies' man."

"Don't believe the hype," Riley said, taking a sip of water. Though there was some truth to the statement; he had left a trail of more than a few broken hearts in Manhattan.

"I believe what I see, and you've been tagged with lots of women online."

"Doesn't mean I've slept with them all," Riley replied. "Besides, Wynter asked me to sit with her. What was I supposed to do, turn down a grieving woman in her time of need?"

Shay frowned. "Of course not. I just don't want to see her get hurt."

"I have no intention of hurting Wynter," Riley stated. He wanted to spend some time with her, learn what made her tick. And from everything he'd seen thus far, she was a woman worth knowing.

Wynter stood at the far side of the room, away from everyone. It had been a long day and just as difficult as she'd imagined it would be. Laying her aunt to rest had taken every ounce of strength she possessed. Although she felt mentally and emotionally exhausted, physically, she felt *alive*. It was as if all her senses were heightened.

Because Riley was here.

Not here literally, because while one of her aunt's friends had been giving their condolences she'd lost sight of him, but she knew he was on the premises. He wouldn't leave without saying goodbye. Wynter didn't know how she knew this. She just did. It was as if they were tethered together by some invisible cord.

Wynter feared the only way they'd break it was if they crossed the line of intimacy, but Riley had been a perfect gentleman and companion. She hadn't known what she was going to say outside the church, but when she said she wanted him by her side, intuitively, she had known it was the right thing. Riley had been a shoulder, a rock all day, and she would be forever grateful. And if given the chance, she might show him how much she appreciated him.

"Earth to Wynter." Egypt snapped her fingers in front of Wynter's face.

Wynter blinked. "What?"

"You were daydreaming," Egypt responded, "and if I had to guess who about, I would say that fine specimen of tall, dark and chocolate who's been by your side today."

Wynter chuckled nervously. "Who, Riley?" If anyone could ferret the truth out of her, it was Egypt. She was a natural lie detector and always seemed to know when Wynter was telling a fib. At five foot ten, Egypt was tall, beautiful and buxom in dark slacks and a black wraparound silk shirt that showed off her cleavage. Wynter loved her confidence and often wished she could imitate it.

"Don't act coy now," Egypt replied with a saucy grin. "I done peeped you two. Heck, we all did, because the man has been glued to your side."

"He's being a good friend."

"Who wants to get in your pants."

"Egypt!" Wynter pulled Egypt away from the crowd. "You can't talk like that. What if someone heard you?"

"So what?" Egypt shrugged with a smirk. "You've always cared much too much about what other people think."

Egypt was never afraid to speak her mind. It was one of the many traits of hers Wynter admired, but in this instance, she would rather Riley not find out she might still harbor the itty-bittiest of crushes on him.

"I do not."

"Yes, you do," Egypt said emphatically. "So, when are you going to stop worrying about them?"

"Starting now," Wynter stated. "My father cut me off."

"Really?"

"Yep. He wants me back at Barrington Investments. Since I refused, he told me I'll have to support myself if I choose to keep traveling and working on my blog."

"Good for them."

"Egypt!" Wynter couldn't believe her friend was being so unkind.

"Quite frankly, I think this is exactly the kick in the butt you need to get you out of your rut. Your writing is amazing. You have a gift for lifestyle and travel articles. You're truly talented, Wynter, but you've always hidden behind your family's wealth. Now you'll be forced to put a little more time and effort into your dream. That's not necessarily a bad thing. Look at it on the positive side. Without your dad's purse, you have the freedom to do things your way. You're not beholden to anyone."

"I guess I never thought about it like that." Wynter had thought about everything she wouldn't have, not what she stood to gain. That was why she needed her friends around; they gave her perspective.

"When I was working as a sous chef for other people, I hated it," Egypt said. "Now I have my food truck. I'm the owner, manager and chef. I make the final decisions. And now you will, too."

Egypt was right. She could do this. She was already on her way. Once she had more subscribers, the advertising dollars and sponsors would come.

"Now, don't think you've fooled me because we changed topics," Egypt said. "I want to know about you and Riley."

"So do I," Asia said, sliding closer to them. Wynter hadn't even seen the petite diva come up. At five foot two, with a blunt, straight bob and wearing an off-the-shoulder black dress and knee-high black boots, Asia had a firecracker personality and was always the life of the party. In Asia's case, big things came in small packages. "You two have been awfully cozy today."

"That's right." Before Wynter knew it, Lyric had joined their group of three and wrapped her arms around Wynter's shoulder. Lyric was more subtle and reserved than Egypt and Asia. Her café au lait complexion and almond-shaped eyes bore a subtle hint of makeup, as was appropriate for a service, while her lithe ballerina's figure was ensconced in a simple black V-neck sheath dress. Her long auburn hair was in a sleek ponytail.

"Listen, there is nothing going on between Riley and me," Wynter responded.

"Not yet," Egypt surmised, "but I see you." She pointed her index and middle fingers at herself and back at Wynter.

"My aunt just passed away and…"

"And you need someone to help ease the pain?" Asia chuckled coyly, placing her hand over her mouth.

Wynter laughed. "You guys are terrible, you know that?"

"We might be, but you love us," Egypt replied.

And Wynter did. Having her friends present made the day bearable. Now she just had to get through the reading of her aunt's will. And she suspected that was why her aunt's lawyer, Sidney Carter, a salt-and-pepper-haired gentleman wearing a bespoke suit, was coming toward her.

"Ms. Barrington, it's that time," Sidney said. "And are you ladies Egypt Cox, Lyric Taylor and Asia Reynolds?"

"We are," all three women said in unison.

"And where might Shay Davis and Teagan Williams be?" he asked.

"Right behind you," Teagan responded, lifting her hand. Her friend was always professional and, today, she sported a black pantsuit and chic short haircut. Her caramel skin gleamed and her makeup was top-notch, but then again, that was Teagan. "And who wants to know?"

Sidney cleared his throat. "Pardon the interruption, but the five of you have been asked to attend the reading of Helaine Smith's will along with Ms. Barrington."

"So, you're Mr. Carter," Teagan responded. "You left a message with my assistant confirming that I was attending the funeral."

Sidney nodded. "Yes, ma'am. I called each of you." He looked around at each of the five women.

Wynter was surprised as each of the women shrugged. It was the first time she was hearing of the request. "They've been invited? Why?"

"More will follow during the reading of the will," Sidney replied and motioned ahead of him. "Would you all mind coming with me? The rest of your family is headed to the study."

"I honestly have no idea," Egypt said. "I assumed

when he called maybe it had something to do with the head count for food."

Several of the ladies laughed, but they followed Wynter in a single file out of the living room and down the hall to the study. Her parents were already seated on the sofa, while Corey and Francesca sat in adjacent chairs.

"What is your posse doing here?" Corey inquired, folding his arms across his chest. "This is for family only."

"Posse?" Egypt asked. "If it wasn't your aunt's funeral, I'd take off my hoops and show you a posse, Corey."

Her brother rolled his eyes and his wife scoffed as if her friends were being uncouth. *Whatever*, Wynter thought. She wanted to get this over with so she could move on to the next phase in her life.

"I've asked Ms. Barrington's friends to attend," Sidney responded. He shuffled behind her father's desk and took a seat. Opening his briefcase, he pulled out a blue document.

"I don't understand why," her mother replied. "They aren't family."

"Bear with me, Mrs. Barrington. You'll understand in a moment. Shall we begin?"

Sidney began reading. "'I, Helaine Smith, being of sound mind and memory'—"

"Excuse me, Mr. Carter, but if you don't mind, there's no need to read all the fluff," her father interjected. "Can you get to the heart of the matter?"

"Why is everyone in such a rush? Aunt Helaine has only been buried a few hours. Can't you show some respect?" Wynter cried. She didn't realize she had verbalized her statement until her family looked at her in shock. They weren't used to her speaking up, let alone speaking out. Properly chastened, the room quieted and Sidney continued.

He read the special requests and donations her aunt was giving to her favorite charities, but when it came to her personal belongings, everyone sat a little straighter in their chairs. "I leave my jewelry and all the artwork to my sister, Melinda Barrington,'" Sidney stated.

"That's it?" her mother asked. "What about the house?"

Sidney sighed in exasperation, but he continued. "'I leave my home and all its remaining possessions to my niece, Wynter Barrington. You were like the daughter I never had, and now you will always have a home no matter where you are.'"

"Wynter!" Corey said, jumping up out of his chair. "But what about me? I'm her nephew." He looked at the lawyer. "Is there nothing for me?"

"If you will allow me to finish," Sidney huffed impertinently.

"Carry on." Her mother fluttered her hand in the air.

"'As to the personal wealth that I've garnered, I leave two hundred fifty thousand to my longtime housekeeper, Hope, and her husband, Mark Nelson. To Egypt Cox, Lyric Taylor, Asia Reynolds, Shay Davis and Teagan Williams—you girls have always been kind to an old woman and were like daughters to me. You treated my Wynter like the queen she is. I leave each of you two hundred thousand dollars to help you pursue your dreams of starting your own business.'"

"What?" Her brother looked absolutely poleaxed.

"She's giving it to them!" He pointed at Wynter's friends. "That's a million dollars! She must have been out of her mind. I mean, really, loony tunes."

"I will not have you speak that way about Aunt Helaine," Wynter stated.

Corey snorted. "What do you care? You got the house."

Sidney cleared his throat. "I'm afraid that's not all. Miss Smith acquired a substantial fortune worth several million after she and Melinda sold their family business."

"Although I don't agree with my sister giving these ladies that kind of money," her mother said, leaning back, "surely I'll be inheriting the rest. Isn't that right, Mr. Carter?" Her dark brown eyes landed on the attorney.

"I'm afraid not, ma'am," he replied and picked up the document. "'I leave the remainder of my estate to my niece, Wynter Barrington.'"

Shocked gasps echoed throughout the room, including from Wynter.

"What did you say?" her mother asked, tilting her head to regard him. "Are you telling me my own sister cut me out of her will and left everything to my daughter?"

"Not exactly, Mrs. Barrington. As you're aware, your sister named you as beneficiary on her life insurance policy to help pay for the funeral expenses and any debts and taxes Helaine may have owed. Further, Ms. Smith has made you the executor of her will. I trust you can fulfill these duties?"

"Oh, my God!" Her mother clutched her chest. "I can't believe this. My sister and I are the only Smiths left. She wouldn't exclude me and leave me trinkets, art and a small life insurance policy. Not when her personal wealth came from the sale of our family business."

Sidney huffed. "A quarter of a million dollars is not small, Mrs. Barrington."

"What did you do, Wynter?" Corey asked, rushing toward Wynter. Fury blazed across his light brown features. "You cozy up to the old lady so she'd leave you everything?"

"Back off, Corey!" Egypt stepped in front of Wynter, because she was too shell-shocked to move. Aunt Helaine had essentially left her everything she owned. It seemed unreal. One minute she was thinking about how she was going to survive, and the next she was a multimillionaire.

"Or what?" Corey inquired, puffing out his chest. "What are you going to do, Egypt? Matter of fact, why don't you and your girl group leave? I think you've done enough for one day."

"Not only were they asked to be here by the attorney, but they are here for me," Wynter responded hotly, finding her voice.

"When was this drafted?" her mother inquired, peering at Mr. Carter. "My sister wasn't well the last couple of years."

"Ma'am, Ms. Smith was of sound mind and body when she wrote this will a few years ago," Sidney replied.

"We'll see about that." Melinda rose to her feet. "I'm challenging this will."

"Mother!" Wynter quickly moved to her side. "Why would you do that? You would be going against Aunt

Helaine's wishes. Is that really what you want to do? If the money is that important to you, surely we can figure this out as a family?"

Her mother grasped Wynter by the shoulders. "Wynter, I know you mean well, but do you have any idea of the magnitude of your aunt's wealth? You're ill-equipped to handle it."

"And you aren't?" Wynter snapped.

"Your mother is right," her father said, coming to his wife's aid and wrapping an arm around her shoulder. "You're always gallivanting across the world, and there will be matters to attend to. *We*—" he looked down at her mother "—can address them."

"Clearly, Aunt Helaine felt otherwise," Wynter replied. "And I will fight for what's mine." She turned to Sidney. "Mr. Carter, legally, the house is mine until the court states otherwise, is that correct?"

"Yes, Ms. Barrington."

"Because that's where me—" Wynter turned to her best friends, who had remained silent during the exchange "—and my *girl group* will be staying, since it's obvious I'm not welcome here." She already had keys to her aunt's home yet hadn't been able to bring herself to go alone, but she wasn't alone now. "C'mon." She looked at Egypt, Lyric, Asia, Shay and Teagan. "Let's go."

Her mother wrenched out of her father's arms. "Wynter, stop this!" She blocked Wynter's path. "I don't want to fight you, but I will. I will not let you squander my family's legacy."

Wynter faced her mother. She was tired of being pushed around. "Bring it on." Then she stepped from around her mother and exited the study with her friends behind her.

She heard her mother yell, "I will bury you in paperwork. Neither you nor your friends will see a dime of that money!"

Wynter didn't turn back around. Instead, she kept walking. She focused on putting one foot in front of the other before the tears stinging her eyes fell. She had to get to her room, get her belongings and get the hell out of this house. She refused to take abuse from her family a moment longer. She'd buried the most important person in her life, and when she was feeling at her lowest, adrift without any support, she'd learned her aunt hadn't left her at all. She'd given her a home and the financial wherewithal to fulfill her wildest dreams. But Wynter would give it all away in a heartbeat if she could have her aunt back.

Now she would have to fight her entire family for the privilege of keeping what was rightfully hers. But they'd underestimated Wynter. They had no idea what she was capable of when push came to shove—but they were about to find out.

# Four

It was time for Riley to go home. He'd done a good deed by standing by Wynter, but the funeral was over and the family had moved on to the reading of the will. He was about to throw in the towel when he saw the Six Gems striding down the hall. The heartbroken look on Wynter's faced brooked no discussion. He went to Shay instead and pulled her aside while the other women rushed up the stairs behind Wynter.

His eyes pierced Shay's. "What happened?"

"The Barrington family," Shay hissed, pulling him into a corner. "They're terrible. If you could have seen how they treated Wynter. It was horrible, Riley."

His brow furrowed. "On a day like today? Why? They should be sticking together as a family."

Shay rolled her shoulders upward and then glanced

around to be sure no one was listening. "Because Wynter's aunt—she left Wynter nearly everything, the house and most of her money. Plus, get this, Riley—" she paused several beats as she sucked in a deep breath "—her aunt left each of us Six Gems two hundred thousand to pursue our dreams of opening up our own businesses."

"What?" he asked, his voice rising.

"Wynter's mother is furious. Claimed Wynter must have done something to sway her aunt to leave her everything and leave her mother nothing."

"Her own mother said that?" Riley couldn't believe what he was hearing. How could Wynter's mother turn on her like that?

"She vowed to contest the will. Sounds like she's prepared to fight Wynter to the death for that money."

"Unfortunately, death doesn't bring out the best in people," Riley stated. He'd done a stint in inheritance law when he'd been an intern in law school. He'd been surprised by how families turned on one another for the sake of the almighty dollar. "Well, I hope Wynter knows she's not alone and that we'll do all we can to help her."

"We?" Shay asked, cocking her head to regard him. "Why are you so buddy-buddy with my girl?"

"I'm not. I told you, we're old friends who caught up." He hated lying to his sister, but he wasn't ready to define whatever was going on between him and Wynter. He wanted it to evolve naturally and without artifice.

Shay didn't look like she believed him one bit, but she let it go when Wynter came down the stairs moments later, carrying a suitcase. Egypt was behind her, carrying an oversize duffel bag over her shoulder and a laptop bag.

Wynter walked out into the cool January night air. Once outside, she turned to them as they gathered around her. "That was very difficult. You have no idea how much. Just know that I appreciate you all."

"And we love you," Egypt responded, which brought a smile to Wynter's somber expression.

"But, if you don't mind, I'm going to need some company at my aunt's place."

"Give me a second to check out of my hotel," Teagan replied, "and I'll be there in a flash."

"Same here," Asia said. "We've got you."

"So do I," Riley replied, surprising himself when he said the words out loud. He hadn't meant to, but he felt compelled, and not because Wynter was a woman he was attracted to, but because it was the right thing to do. Wynter glanced up as if she were coming out of a fog and had just noticed him standing there. "I'll do everything I can to help you with your legal case."

He watched her swallow, and then she said, "Thank you. Shay, do you mind taking me to Aunt Helaine's?"

"Of course not," Shay replied and gave Riley a suspecting look before rushing off.

With this newest development, Riley didn't know what might happen between him and Wynter, but he knew they were intrinsically joined, and he wasn't ready to separate until their relationship reached its natural conclusion. All he had to do was wait.

Wynter felt like she was in self-preservation mode. She'd had to get out of the Barrington house before she went nuclear. Did her family honestly think she was some evil mastermind who had convinced her aunt to leave her everything? The only thing she ever did was love Helaine. Love her like a daughter, and, in the end, that was exactly how her aunt felt. Wynter was the daughter she'd never had, and hearing those words meant everything.

But more surprising than the announcement of her inheritance were her interactions with Riley. From the moment she ran into him at the River Walk, she could feel a palpable energy between them. It was an awareness between a man and a woman and not the friendship vibes she'd felt in the past.

Wynter didn't know what to make of it, and apparently, neither did Shay, because she questioned Wynter on the drive to Helaine's. "What's going on between you and my brother?" Shay asked point-blank.

Wynter turned to her. "I don't understand."

"C'mon. Don't act coy. There is definitely a vibe between the two of you."

"I'm not saying there isn't," Wynter replied honestly, "but if there were, would that bother you?"

"You betcha!" Shay responded quickly. "Riley likes playing the field and isn't interested in settling down with one woman. And you? Wynter, you wear your heart on your sleeve, and I would hate to see you get hurt by getting involved with my brother. Will you stay away from him?"

Wynter received Shay's message loud and clear: *hands off!*

And she wanted to heed her best friend's advice because she understood everything Shay said. After their walk the other day, she'd read up about Riley's reputation online, but that didn't stop her wayward heart from wanting to know if Riley felt the same pulse, the same kinetic energy she felt when he was near.

"Well?" Shay asked. "Are you going to answer me?"

"Riley has been a great friend to me today and the other day, when he happened to find me crying in public. I hardly think that's making a play for me. I don't think I should have to keep my distance."

Shay gave her a rueful smile as she drove. "My brother is great in the clutch, always has been, but he doesn't stick around. When we were growing up, he always took care of me and Mama. Until I was older, I had no idea my mother had any sort of mental health issues. It wasn't until Riley went to college and his calls and visits became less frequent that I realized how much he'd been holding inside. So, trust me when I say this—don't pin all your hopes and dreams on Riley. He will let you down."

"Sounds like you speak from experience," Wynter replied, giving her friend a sideways glance.

"I don't blame him for pursuing his passion," Shay said, and at Wynter's disbelieving look, she continued, "I don't. I wish I would have known a little sooner and been prepared for what awaited me once he left."

Wynter nodded. She would have to remember Shay's advice. Otherwise, she could be in a world of hurt if she allowed herself to go down the rabbit hole with Riley.

Hours later, Wynter, Egypt, Shay, Teagan, Asia and Lyric were in their pajamas and nightshirts, cuddled in blankets on the floor of her aunt Helaine's seven-bedroom, seven-and-a-half-bath house in Elm Creek.

Once they had arrived, they'd been greeted by Hope, Aunt Helaine's live-in housekeeper, who'd returned to the house after the service and hadn't heard of Wynter's aunt's bequest. Hope had been shocked to hear she'd received an inheritance, and even though she didn't have to, Hope had ensured the bedrooms for Wynter and her friends were set up and scrounged up some light snacks.

The housekeeper's version of "light" included a charcuterie board of thick-cut salami, prosciutto, Gouda, brie and herb-flavored cream cheeses, fig jam, pepper jelly, cornichons, water crackers, nuts, and an assortment of fruit. It had been difficult to eat after the service, so the snacks were welcomed by all.

"It's so nice to have all you guys here," Wynter said. Wearing her favorite cotton pajamas, she settled her back against the sofa in her aunt's living room. "I remember having our pajama parties here."

"So do I," Egypt quipped after having changed into a tank maxi sleep shirt. "Your aunt would make it an event, with popcorn and pizza and hot baked cookies. I'd forgotten how much I missed this place."

"How are you feeling?" Lyric asked. Her long auburn hair was in a messy updo, and she was dressed in jogger pants and a cropped top. Wynter would kill for her sleek dancer's body.

"Still in disbelief," Wynter replied honestly. "It felt like I was having an out-of-body experience. It was as if I was watching the reading of the will, but I wasn't present."

"I felt your mother's displeasure that your aunt

deigned to give us anything," Teagan replied with a frown. Teagan had opted for long satin pajamas. "She's always been tightly strung, but this was a whole new low."

"How *low* can you go?" Egypt said with a laugh. "You mind passing me more of that wine, Teagan?" She held up her empty wineglass.

Teagan and Asia had brought several bottles of wine with them, because they'd known Wynter was going to need something strong to help take the sting out of her family's harsh treatment of her.

While Teagan filled Egypt's glass, Egypt asked, "So, what do we do now? Should we all—" she glanced at the other women in the room "—move forward with opening our own businesses, or should we prepare for battle?"

"That's a good question," Wynter said. "I need to talk to Riley, since it appears my mother is serious about contesting the will."

"She believes you conspired to steal her family legacy," Asia stated bluntly.

Wynter jumped to her feet. "And that's utterly ridiculous." She looked down at the other women. "When would I have had the time? I've been traveling and writing. This has me shook."

Shay rose from the floor and came over to wrap her arms around Wynter. "You're not in this alone."

"I know that here," Wynter said, pointing to her temple, "but tell that to my heart." She patted her chest. "My entire family is against me." Tears slid down her cheeks. She leaned her head on Shay's shoulder and let them fall. "It's so unfair."

"Yes, it is." Teagan placed her wineglass on the cocktail table and stood up. "But we will fight with you."

"Against my family?" Wynter asked, lifting her head.

"If necessary," Asia replied. "Your aunt wanted you to have this house—" she motioned her arms around the room "—and to have that money. They've no right to circumvent her wishes."

Egypt walked toward Wynter and softly grabbed her chin, forcing Wynter to look up at her. "And we won't let them. First thing tomorrow, we fight. Ain't that right?"

Wynter nodded.

"I can't hear you!" Egypt cried.

"That's right," Wynter replied, this time a little louder and a whole lot stronger. "I will fight for what's mine." She would get what was due her, even if she had to fight the entire Barrington family.

# Five

On Sunday, Riley woke early and hit the hotel's gym for nearly two hours of cardio and weights. He even did a few hours of work, going over case files. Now he was ready to face the task he'd been avoiding since arriving in San Antonio nearly a week ago —it was time to see his mother. Although work and the funeral had kept him busy, the real reason he'd shied away was because he'd needed to prepare himself.

He had to be in the right head space when he visited his mom. He never knew which Eliza Davis he was going to find. Was it happy Eliza, who was thrilled to see her successful lawyer son? Or was it depressed Eliza, who couldn't get out of bed, much less comb her hair or shower? He had to be prepared for whichever version he encountered.

He'd had a lot of practice dealing with her mood

swings. Back then, she hadn't been officially diagnosed as a manic depressive. However, once he had been making good money at his first law firm, Riley had been determined to ensure his mother received the best care. But despite that, she didn't always take her medication as prescribed, which meant her moods fluctuated.

After showering, he changed into jeans, a pullover sweater and a leather jacket, and he drove the Bentley, which had arrived a few days ago, to the Heights at Stone Oak, a gated subdivision that had tennis and basketball courts, as well as a swimming pool and jogging trails. He'd moved his mother and Shay there once he became one of the top lawyers on the East Coast. It had been difficult uprooting his mother from the familiar house she'd known for nearly twenty years, but once she saw the big backyard with room for a garden and tranquil koi pond, she'd been thrilled.

He pulled the car into the driveway and looked around. He'd done good by his family, though he was sure they might say different because his trips home were infrequent. Riley ensured they had everything they could need: a nurse, a lawn service and a housekeeper who came once a week to keep the place tidy. It was the least he could do, but now that he was back in San Antonio permanently, he intended to pitch in.

Turning off the engine, he sauntered to the front of the house and used his key. "Hello!" he called out.

Several seconds later, his mother came bounding down the stairs in jeans and a pullover sweater. Her dark brown hair was brushed back into a ponytail, and her dark eyes were bright and clear. It was going to be a good day. "Riley!" She rushed into his arms. Having his mother hug him back was a good feeling.

Riley hadn't realized how much he needed today to be a good day until he saw her smiling face beaming up at him. At five foot six, she was a few heads shorter than he was. "Hey, Mom, how are you?"

"Fabulous, now that you're here." A warm glow suffused her medium-brown cheeks. "Would you like something to drink? I was about to head back to the garden."

"A drink sounds great." Riley followed her inside toward the back of the house, which had a large eat-in kitchen and butcher-block island. He watched as she opened the double-sided refrigerator and pulled out a beer for him.

He raised a brow because he couldn't remember his mother keeping alcohol on hand, but he accepted the drink. He screwed off the top and took a swig.

"Don't give me that look, Riley," his mother said. "I don't drink, and you know Shay is a health nut."

"Then whose is this?" He held up the beer bottle.

A blush crossed his mother's symmetrical features. "A friend."

"Friend?" he asked, sitting down on one of the wicker bar stools. "As in, the male variety?"

She shrugged. "Is that so wrong? I am entitled."

"Of course you are." Riley was happy to hear she had emerged from the cocoon she'd been in to embrace life once again.

"Darryl is a wonderful man and occasionally while watching a football game, he wants a beer. I keep a six-pack just for him."

Why hadn't Shay told him his mother had a man

in her life? It would certainly have eased his anxiety. He would have to have a word with his sister about it. "Good for you, Ma. I'm glad to see you're doing well."

She sighed and walked over to sit beside him at the island. "I know growing up with a mother like me was challenging for you, Riley. I'm sorry I wasn't there for you. I didn't understand my condition or know how to take care of myself."

"It's okay, Ma. I don't blame you. You have a medical condition."

"All the same, it was a terrible burden to put on you. You didn't get to have a chance to be a teenager because you were always keeping me upright. It wasn't fair."

Riley reached for her hand across the short distance and took it in his own. "I'm glad you're better. That's all I need right now."

"And Shay?" Her mother shook her head. "Caring for me took a toll on her, too, and was the cause of her divorce. And now she doesn't date much. She needs to get out more and make time for herself."

"Now that I'm back, I'll ensure she does."

"And you?" His mother searched his eyes. "What's going on with you on that front?"

He shrugged.

"Riley?" She touched his cheek with her palm. "There's no one special?"

His mind immediately went to Wynter. She was in a vulnerable state, and he wanted to do anything he could to help her. He didn't know why he felt protective over her, but he did. The battle with her parents over her aunt's estate could be long. He doubted she had any idea what was in store. He'd already reached out to the head of the local probate department at his firm.

Then there was the lady herself. She was absolutely not his type. He was used to women who understood the score and could accept an affair. She deserved a man who could give her more, and Riley wasn't it, but that didn't stop him from desiring her. Her beautiful caramel skin and those waves of delicious curls, her figure with the right amount of curves to fit in his palms— He imagined peeling off her clothes, stripping her bare and splaying her beneath him. Would her kissable, full lips part in surrender? Would her eyes flicker with desire as they had that night on the River Walk?

"So, there is someone?" His mother picked up on what he wasn't saying.

He thought about Shay and how she wasn't keen on him spending any time with Wynter. It was best he kept any interaction with Wynter to himself. "There's no one," Riley stated. "I'm too busy with work and getting reacclimated to life in Texas."

"I imagine it's very different from the East Coast."

"Very." Riley laughed. "Why don't you show me this garden? I want to see what you've done with the place."

It would be a good distraction to keep him from picking up the phone and calling Wynter, but he couldn't anyway. Shay had spent the night at Wynter's aunt Helaine's house, and if he were to call, she would surely snoop into his affairs. Because that was certainly what was going to happen between him and Wynter. They would have an affair. It was just a matter of when.

"I'm going to miss you," Wynter said as Egypt, Lyric, Asia and Teagan stood outside her aunt's home after their suitcases had been loaded into the hired Escalade idling nearby, ready to take them to the airport. Having her best friends for the weekend had been just what the doctor ordered, but now they were going back to their lives and careers. Careers Wynter hoped would blossom once she could assure them they would receive the gifts her aunt left them in the will.

"We're going to miss you, too." Asia leaned in for a tight squeeze of Wynter's shoulders before moving away so Lyric could hug her.

"I know we might be far, but we're only a phone call away anytime you need us," Lyric stated, grasping both sides of Wynter's face. "Remember that, okay?"

Tears welled in Wynter's eyes, and she nodded.

"Okay, let's not get all sentimental," Egypt fussed, breaking the trio apart. "Y'all acting like we're not going to see each other. We have our annual girls' trip in Barbados this year!"

Teagan snapped her fingers. "That's right, and it's going to be the bomb, just like Vegas was last year! Wynter, we can't thank you enough for always finding affordable deals and giving us a payment schedule. You're our personal travel agent." She did have a knack for planning getaways, something she enjoyed incorporating into *Wynter's Corner*.

Wynter chuckled. "You're welcome. Once you see the villa I've got, it's going to blow your minds."

The women chuckled, and after a few more hugs and kisses, they slid into the vehicle and drove away. Wynter sighed audibly.

"It's going to be okay," Shay said, patting her hand.

"I know it will," Wynter replied. Before the fiasco at

the will reading on Saturday, she'd come to the realiza-
tion she was going to have to put on her big-girl panties
and figure out her next move. Over the weekend, she'd
discussed with her friends that it was best they didn't
count on the money until the will was settled. In the
interim, the ladies would work on their business plans
and getting everything in order in preparation for when
the matter was resolved.

Wynter would work on building her blog and gar-
nering the followers she needed to ensure its success.
It would be difficult, but she was going to do it. The
first thing she needed to do was find an estate lawyer.

But one name dominated her thoughts.

Riley Davis.

He was gorgeous, sexy and superbly male. Heat
spilled over Wynter's skin just thinking about how he'd
held her during her aunt's service. Riley had been the
steadying influence she needed and *wanted*.

Shay had warned Wynter to avoid any dealings with
Riley, and he should be taboo, but that only made Wynter want him more. She was in a quandary. Should she
pursue her heart's desire? Or always wonder if she
imagined the need she'd seen reflected in his dark eyes
as he'd supported her the day of the funeral?

"Wynter?"

Wynter blinked several times and realized Shay was
speaking to her. "Hmm…?"

"I was asking if you wanted me to stay with you tonight?"

Wynter glanced up at the two-story stone house. This
had been her second home, a place of shelter and comfort. She couldn't get into her own head. Her aunt had

wanted this place to be hers. She shook her head. "No, I've got this."

A frown creased Shay's forehead. "Are you sure?"

"Yes," Wynter said. And she was. It was time for her to stand on her own two feet. Starting now.

As he poured himself some brandy in his penthouse, Riley thought back to how the day with his mother had gone. He was pleasantly surprised by the progress she'd made. She was taking her meds and getting the help she needed. Mental illness was something that could be managed with the right care, but his father had turned a blind eye when they'd been married.

He'd been so busy screwing other women behind his mother's back, he hadn't seen the signs. And when he chose to leave, he hadn't looked back to the children he was leaving in her care. Instead, he married again and started a new life, devastating Eliza. She'd already been fragile, so losing her husband had been the straw that broke the camel's back. And now, over two decades later, she was finally the mother he'd always wanted.

Riley sipped his drink as he stared out at the San Antonio skyline. Seeing the demise of his parents' marriage had made Riley want the exact opposite. He didn't want love and commitment. They only brought heartache. Riley was happy with the here and now. His relationships with women were short-lived, and that was exactly the way he wanted it.

But he did want Wynter Barrington, his sister's best friend. He wanted a scorching-hot night with the sultry woman with the wavy hair and an ass that was made for squeezing. Shay was adamantly against him getting involved with Wynter in any way, shape or form, but Wynter was a grown woman. Surely she could make her own decisions? If Wynter gave him the slightest indication she was interested, Riley doubted he could resist the invitation.

His cell phone rang suddenly, and Riley swiped his thumb across to answer. "Hello."

"Riley, hi. It's Wynter."

"I know who it is," he responded. He recognized her voice. "How are you?"

"I could be better," Wynter said. "And that's where you come in."

"Oh, yeah?" He couldn't resist smiling. "How can I help?"

"I was hoping we could meet tomorrow at your office and discuss my aunt's will in further detail. Are you available?"

Damn. Riley had been hoping for dinner and maybe adjourning to his place. He mentally ticked off the appointments he had scheduled for tomorrow. "It would have to be later, around 3:00 p.m., if that works for you?"

"Oh, yes, that's wonderful. I really appreciate you fitting me in."

"I told you I would help you in any way I could," he responded.

She chuckled softly. "I know, but sometimes people say that when you're grieving, but they're only being kind. They don't actually expect you to call."

"*I* meant it."

"Thank you," Wynter said. "It's nice to have someone in my corner."

Riley was hoping that wasn't all she wanted, but all too quickly, after he gave her directions to his office, Wynter terminated the call. He would have preferred to talk to her longer, but he didn't want to push. He had to be sure Wynter was as interested as he was in pursuing a deeper connection, but he would have to wait to find out.

Riley groaned. It was going to be a long night, spent dreaming about having Wynter underneath him.

# Six

Wynter gazed up at the imposing skyscraper, her heart pounding about her meeting with Riley. After all these years, her schoolgirl crush had turned into full-on attraction. However, she wasn't here to act on those feelings, especially because she didn't want to ruin her friendship with Shay.

Although she could have gone to Sidney Carter, the lawyer who'd read the will, Riley was someone she trusted, and Wynter was hoping he could lead her in the right direction when it came to her mother contesting her aunt's will. She hadn't heard from her family since the funeral on Saturday, and that was disheartening. They truly believed she had coerced her aunt into leaving her the lion's share of her estate.

Pushing aside her nerves, Wynter walked swiftly

across the polished marble floor of the lobby toward the bank of stainless-steel elevators. Pushing the up button, she waited for the elevator to take her to Jamison, Charles and Davis, Riley's new law office.

Moments later, she was exiting the elevator and walking toward the U-shaped reception desk, where a beautiful brunette with an impeccable updo sat. Wynter glanced down at her outfit. Underneath her peacoat, she wore a pencil skirt and a long-sleeved button-down silk top that flared out with a waterfall of ruffles. She looked smart and sophisticated and worthy of being there.

"May I help you?" the brunette asked.

"Wynter Barrington. I have an appointment with Riley Davis."

"Of course—I'll get him right away. Please have a seat."

Nodding, Wynter made her way to an expensive-looking group of armchairs and sat down. Wynter removed her coat. She was nervous, and not about the matter of fighting her family for her inheritance, but because she was meeting with Riley. During their past two encounters, he'd been kind to her, but there had been something—a gossamer-fine thread—connecting them that was about more than comfort.

Wynter felt the hairs on the back of her neck rise and looked up to see Riley in front of her. How long had he been standing there, watching? She didn't know. She just knew that with the sunlight streaming in from the floor-to-ceiling windows, he looked extraordinarily delicious. He was clean-shaven and wore a dark blue pinstriped suit with a silver tie. He looked every bit the high-powered divorce attorney.

His dark eyes locked on hers, and Wynter felt something unravel inside her.

"Wynter, it's good to see you." Riley offered her his hand.

She curved hers around it, and a jolt of electricity rushed through her fingertips. His grip was firm as he helped her up, and her heart skipped a beat. She suspected Riley's hands knew how to stir and torment a woman's body to the point of release. "Thank you for seeing me."

"Of course." He smiled and released her hand, but Wynter's heart was thumping so hard in her chest, she could feel it in her ribs. "Let's go to my office."

Mutely, Wynter followed him, and in doing so, got a view of his broad shoulders and tapered waist as he walked ahead of her. Riley was fit, and it showed in the way he wore his clothes. Before she knew it, they were stopping in front of a glass corner office. Riley allowed her to precede him before joining her.

"Please have a seat." He motioned to the sofa as opposed to the chair in front of his large desk. She was hoping Riley would sit behind it and give her some breathing room, but instead, he was going for a more casual approach. When he pushed a button on his desk and the glass in his office went from clear to opaque, her heart began to pound against her rib cage. No one would see them. They would have complete privacy.

Wynter tried not think about what that meant. Instead, she sat on one end of the soft, plush beige sofa, while Riley, after unbuttoning his jacket, sat on the other side.

"So," he began, crossing a muscular leg over his knee, "I assume you're here about the will?"

Wynter struggled to think, because all she saw were his thick, toned thighs. She wondered what it would feel like if she straddled him. She blinked. She had to stop this. *Focus.* She glanced up and found he was looking at her expectantly.

She swallowed thickly. "As you know, my family was very unhappy after the reading of my aunt's will, and they've vowed to contest it. I can only assume they have engaged counsel—or *will*—and I have to do the same. I need to know how to fight them and what my options are."

He nodded. "Contesting your aunt's will is going to be time-consuming and expensive for your parents. The burden of proof is on them to show you coerced your aunt, had some undue influence or that the will was improperly prepared or executed, and they'll need to find witnesses who can support that claim."

"That's crazy, Riley. There's no one who will say I unduly influenced her. Everyone knows how close we were."

Riley sat upright. "That's great, because your main priority will be showing your aunt was of sound mind and body when the will was executed."

Wynter nodded. "My aunt wasn't mentally incapacitated."

"Good. We have a great estate division here that handles these sorts of cases, and I can refer you to one of them."

"Refer me?" Wynter's voice rose slightly. "You can't handle my case yourself?"

Riley shook his head. "Wynter, I'm a divorce law-yer, and I'm damn good one because I stay in my lane. I don't know the nuances of estate law, and you need someone who does. I would be remiss if I didn't refer you to someone else. Given that we're friends as well, that would make you being a client problematic."

Her mouth formed an O. She hadn't realized that, but then again, she didn't know anything about the law. "All right, I would appreciate that, thank you." She rose to her feet and lowered her lashes. She'd been so eager to spend some time with Riley that she hadn't done her research. She felt foolish. "I'm sorry. I won't take up any more of your time."

"You're not. I wanted to see you again."

Wynter glanced furtively up at the man who stood opposite her. His words were provocative. Had he meant them to be? Once again, she felt that strange, unsettling wave of attraction. Suddenly, her mouth became dry and her cheeks felt warm. "You did?"

"Yes." He walked toward her, not in her personal space, but close enough that she could feel his heat, see the black of his irises and have his scent tease her nostrils. He smelled of spice, wood and amber. It was a heady fragrance, and Wynter wanted to taste him. Her eyes immediately went to his lips, and her heart began to race.

And when she glanced up, she was lost.

Riley didn't know why he said it. He could have let Wynter leave his office and she would have been none the wiser to how he felt, but he couldn't. He'd seen the disappointment in her eyes when he told her he couldn't be her attorney. But was there more? He sensed there might be, so he was honest and told her he wanted to see her again.

And now, he caught the look of heat in her brown eyes, because she was looking at his mouth like she wanted what he wanted, which was to taste her.

Getting involved with Wynter could be a mistake, he told himself. His sister was dead set against this, but Riley didn't care. Wynter's scent was filling his head, and she was leaning closer to him. Unable to stop himself, he fused his mouth with hers.

The kiss was soft and tender at first as he acquainted himself with her mouth. Her lips were soft and pillowy, and she tasted sweet, like warm honey. The encounter took a turn when she pressed her full, round breasts against his chest. When he felt Wynter's hand slide up over the muscles of his back, he framed her face with his hands and deepened the kiss, wanting more.

And she gave it to him, parting her lips to let his tongue slide between them. His hand curved around her waist, pulling her closer. His body erupted. He felt hot and hard, as if he were forged from fire—all because of *this* woman. A woman he shouldn't want but couldn't deny he did. She moved against him so that the hard ridge of his erection was pressing against her lower half.

She felt so good. He ran his hands down the contours of her body, and his fingers itched to explore the rest of her.

"Riley…" she whispered, and it was enough to drag his mind back to the present situation.

Had he lost his mind? He was at work!

He stepped away from her so fast, he felt light-headed

with desire. His body was protesting at the speed with which he moved, but all he could do was stare back into her wide and desire-glazed eyes. She touched her swollen lips. "I—I don't know how that happened."

It happened because they were both attracted to each other, and now Riley knew it wasn't one-sided. Wynter wanted him, too. "And yet it did."

Wynter smoothed down the hem of her skirt, which somehow had risen to her thighs during their encounter. Had he done that? He saw a hint of caramel skin as she quickly righted it. "I should go. You'll send me the name of that attorney?"

He nodded, and she was nearly at the door when Riley rushed over. "We should meet again."

She glanced behind her. "Do you really think that's wise?"

Hell yeah, he did. There was no way they could refute the sexual attraction between them, so why try and suppress it? "I do. Meet me for dinner. *Tonight*."

Wynter whirled around at the demanding tone of his words.

He added, "*Please.* I want to see you again. Please—say yes."

Wynter looked down, and Riley thought she was going to deny him, but then she said, "Yes."

"I'll pick you up around seven. That sound good?"

She nodded and then quickly slipped around him and out the door. Riley took a breath and leaned against the glass door. He wouldn't be able to keep his promise to Shay to stay away from Wynter, even though she was forbidden fruit. When he tasted her, he'd lost control to the point where he'd forgotten common sense. They were in his place of work, yet he'd wanted to take Wynter up against the desk and bury himself deep inside her.

Riley scrubbed his face with his hands. He had to get a grip. Once they consummated their relationship, he would be able to ease the ache he felt. Only then could life go back to normal.

Wynter sat in her car in the parking garage, stunned by what had happened upstairs. She'd gone to Riley for help on fighting her parents for her inheritance. She'd never imagined they would end up kissing.

And what a kiss!

Riley kissed like a man who knew what to do with his mouth and tongue. Lord, Wynter could only imagine what he would be like in bed. She wasn't a novice and had enjoyed her sexual encounters with the handful of lovers she'd had, but she suspected being with Riley would be different.

Just kissing him felt different. If they hadn't been in his office, how far would they have gone? All the way? Wynter bit her lip. She should feel shame and regret at her behavior, but she felt elated and aroused because Riley desired her. When he'd run his hands over the curves of her body, she'd wanted him to go underneath her skirt and touch her where she wanted him most. She was still aching.

*Would she let him ease the ache tonight?*

Wynter closed her eyes. Shay's image popped in her mind, cooling her ardor. Her best friend thought it was a mistake for Wynter to get involved with Riley. Was Shay right? Should she give Riley a wide berth because of his playboy reputation?

The thought of canceling their dinner filled Wynter with dread. This was her opportunity to take charge of what she wanted. She refused to be a passive participant in her life any longer. She wanted Riley, and if he wanted her, too, she had to see where this led. She would have to deal with the consequences of her actions on another day.

# Seven

Wynter excitedly dressed for dinner with Riley later that night. She'd already determined she would take the evening as it came. She wasn't going to put any pressure on herself for the night to end one way or the other. However, she also wasn't going to play it safe.

After she left Riley's office, she stopped by her favorite lingerie store and splurged on a sexy bra and panty set so her confidence would be in full bloom for their date. The scalloped edges and floral lace of the panty fit snugly over her bottom, while the deep-V plunging bra was perfect for the cocktail dress she'd chosen, with rhinestone details adorning the low-cut neckline. Wynter sprayed perfume at her touch points, and after pinning up one side of her hair with a rhinestone hair clip, she was ready.

She knew Shay wouldn't approve of this date, but Wynter couldn't ignore her feelings for Riley any longer. And she didn't want to. She understood the risk inherent in dating a playboy like Riley, but this was her chance to see if the spark between them was real. Would it extinguish quickly or light a fire? Wynter had to know. Tonight would be a moment she would always remember.

A gentle knock sounded on the guest room door. Wynter couldn't bear to sleep in her aunt's quarters. It was going to be some time before she would be able to clean out her aunt's things. For now, she needed to focus on her blog and social media content as well as meeting with a lawyer.

Wynter opened the door to find Hope on the other side. "Your guest is here."

"Thank you, Hope. I'm coming down now," Wynter said, grabbing her clutch. Walking down the stairs, she found Riley in the foyer looking resplendent in a dark suit, with a few buttons casually undone on his crisp white shirt. He watched her as she descended. When she reached the last step, Riley strode toward her and offered his hand to assist her.

"Thank you."

Riley's eyes devoured her. "You look incredible."

Wynter smiled. It wasn't often the man you'd admired from the sidelines said you looked beautiful. "So do you."

He gave her a wide grin. "Ready for dinner?"

"Yes."

After helping her into her coat, they exited the house and she slid into his Bentley. When he joined her, Wynter caught another whiff of the spicy scent that was uniquely Riley's. She told herself she wasn't giving up the goodies, but deep down, she knew it was a lie. It was entirely possible that she and Riley would become lovers tonight.

The restaurant was crowded with the usual mix of suave businessmen and glamorous women. Riley's table was set slightly apart from other diners, because he not only wanted the best view, he wanted Wynter all to himself.

All day, when he should have been focusing on his clients' cases, his thoughts had wandered to that mind-blowing kiss they'd shared in his office. He hoped that, after dinner, he would get another taste of this beautiful woman.

Once their dinner choices were made and the wine, poured, he picked up his glass. *"Salut."*

*"Salut."*

The wine was superb, and after she drank a bit, Wynter put down her glass. "Are we going to address the elephant in the room?" she inquired.

His brow quirked. "Are you talking about this afternoon?"

She nodded.

"I equate it to lust. Pure and simple."

Her cheeks flushed at his bold statement.

"Do you always speak so plainly?"

"If you mean, am I always this direct? Then, yes," Riley responded. "I see no reason to beat around the bush. Do you? We find each other attractive."

Wynter chuckled. "That doesn't surprise you? We

grew up together and you never looked at me before. Why now?"

"You're all grown-up," Riley stated, looking at her over the rim of his glass. "We both are free to act on our desires." He took a sip of his wine before placing it on the table. "But to answer your question, you were always a surprise to me, Wynter. Of all of Shay's friends, you weren't afraid to have a conversation with me."

"You don't scare me, Riley Davis."

When she picked up a piece of bread and popped it into her beautiful, delectable mouth, Riley nearly groaned. "Perhaps you should be afraid. I bite."

"I don't mind love bites." A blush crept across her décolletage, and Riley was certain she hadn't meant to say that out loud. But in doing so, she directed his attention to her bosom, which was on lush display in her deep-V-neck rhinestone dress. It might seem demure, with its long sleeves and length that hit at the knee, but it didn't feel that way to Riley. He wanted to rip it off. "I didn't mean to say that."

"You don't mean to do a lot of things around me," Riley stated. "Do I bring out the best or worst in you, I wonder?" He leaned back and regarded her.

"That remains to be seen," Wynter replied cheekily. Their eyes met, hers rebellious and his dark and glinting. Riley realized it was going to be a fun night.

Their meals arrived, and the food was delicious and beautifully presented, though Riley would expect nothing less. His assistant had told him it took months to get a reservation at the restaurant, and the menu prices reflected it.

"How's your mother?" Wynter asked as she worked

on her plate of pan-seared mahi-mahi with cauliflower-broccoli whip and lump crab in white-wine butter.

"She's doing much better than I expected," Riley said, cutting into his Angus steak with butternut squash and truffle puree and a peppery red-wine sauce.

Wynter smiled. "That's wonderful news."

"Yes, it is. I was worried what her condition might be, but she's taking her meds and even seeing someone. I'm glad, because it takes some of the load off Shay. I know it was difficult for Shay when I left home."

"It was." Wynter didn't even try to deny it. "Shay went through a lot with your mother, especially when she was married to Kevin."

"I was against her committing so young."

"Because you yourself refuse to commit?" Wynter asked. "Why is that? Were you hurt in a previous relationship?"

"Whoa!" Riley didn't like being in the hot seat. He didn't like talking about his past, though he doubted he could really call those casual encounters relationships. "Since when did this become the Quiz Riley Show?"

Wynter shrugged. "I'm just trying to get to know you. You're welcome to ask me anything you want."

"Oh, really?" He rubbed his hands together with glee. "Are you ready for the shoe to be on the other foot?"

"I guess that's a no on telling me your reason for remaining single?" Wynter inquired.

The saucy minx was giving it back to him, and Riley found it oddly refreshing. Most women caved to his every whim because they were eager to be with the great Riley Davis. Wynter didn't seem to care at all, and he liked that, but he also wasn't about to talk about other women. It was bad enough she knew about his mother's mental illness.

"You assume right," Riley replied. "And you, why do you travel the world instead of staying at home?"

Wynter chuckled wryly. "You've seen my family, haven't you? We're a hot mess, and this weekend showed we couldn't be farther apart. So, I'm not too keen to stay on the home front. Traveling, aside from providing fodder for my blog, gives me the freedom I love."

"What are you running from?"

"Do I have to be running from something?" she asked sharply and picked up her wineglass and sipped. After setting down her glass, she continued, "Can't I be running *to* something, towards my future? My blog means everything to me. One day, I was so bored with the status quo and doing what others expected of me, I decided to explore and start living my life doing things that were important to me. Traveling is one of those things, and it made me feel like I was a kindred spirit with my aunt. Plus, I found something that I'm really good at, and that speaks to me."

"You're very passionate about it."

"I'm passionate about a lot of things," Wynter responded hotly.

Riley was surprised by Wynter's boldness but didn't mistake her tone. Wynter was up for how he intended the night to end. In fact, if he were a guessing man, he would say she was as eager as he was to move their evening to a different location.

Meeting her again, he'd thought she might be fragile

from losing her aunt and enduring her family's squabbles. How wrong he'd been. He should have remembered the Wynter from his youth, who was impetuous and feisty. When he'd picked her up tonight, his mouth had salivated because the rhinestone dress showcased her mouthwatering body. A body he couldn't wait to see in all its glory, and he would. Tonight.

He called her bluff and gave her a slow, sexy grin. "Care for dessert?"

"Not at all," Wynter said. "I have something else in mind."

He lounged back in the chair, his gaze never leaving hers. "You amaze me, Wynter."

"I hope in a good way?"

"Oh, definitely that," Riley returned. He'd thought she might be skittish about tonight, but Wynter wasn't afraid to let him know exactly what she wanted. What Shay might think about this whole interaction gave him a moment's pause. She would be furious, of course, but Riley would have to take that on the chin, because there was no way he was turning down what Wynter was offering.

He motioned the waiter over. "Check, please."

Wynter stared at her reflection in the mirror of the women's restroom. She couldn't believe how direct she'd been with Riley. There was no way he could mistake that she wanted to spend the night with him. It was a fantasy come true, but she wouldn't play the role of being naive ingenue.

Instead, she was being the aggressor and taking over. Riley was a man she'd wanted for years, and she might not ever get another chance with him. She wasn't about to take a back seat and let him take charge. No, if she was going to do this, it would be on *her* terms.

Losing her aunt had made Wynter see that life was short. She couldn't waste time, because tomorrow wasn't promised. She had to live for today. And who knew if she would ever get another opportunity to be with Riley? Even though she knew this would be one night only and he wasn't offering her a commitment, she had to take her chance, because he hadn't been able to take his eyes off her. She felt the same way—there was something about him that sparked something deep within her.

After powdering her nose and adding another swipe of lipstick, she glanced at herself. Her eyes glittered, and her skin looked flushed with desire. There was no turning back now; she'd laid down the gauntlet, and Wynter couldn't wait to see what happened next.

When she returned to the table, the plates had been cleared. "I'm ready."

Riley's eyes searched hers. For regret? Or a change of heart? He wouldn't find it. She knew what she wanted.

Him.

Riley led Wynter out of the restaurant and to the passenger side of his Bentley, waiting at the curb, and then came round to the driver's side. Before turning on the car, he turned to her. "Are you sure about this, Wynter? Because if we do this, you need to understand that it's only for one night. I don't do commitments or relationships. Besides which, I just became partner at my law firm. I have no room in my life for personal entanglements."

She understood, because she wasn't looking for more than tonight. Her world was already topsy-turvy. Spending the night with Riley would be her choice, something she could control. She was owning her feminine power and taking what she wanted. "Yes, I'm sure. I want you, Riley, but if the feeling isn't mutual..."

He snorted. And before she knew it, Riley's mouth came down hard and demanding on hers. Desire rushed through Wynter as her arms slid around his neck. She returned the kiss and gave him everything. Riley growled against her mouth as he plundered its depths. His tongue mated with hers in an erotic dance that made her belly swoop and dive like a flight of doves taking off. Wynter's mind became frenzied with a blur of sensations. If they didn't stop, she was afraid of what she might let him do right there in the car. Slowly, she pulled away.

He frowned. "Did I come on too strong?"

She shook her head. "Not at all. You were just right, but unless you want to get cited for indecent exposure, I think it might be a good idea for us to take this back to your place."

Riley grinned. "I think you're right." After giving her a heated stare, he turned on the ignition and eased the car out of the parking lot.

The ride to Riley's penthouse at the Alteza, above the Grand Hyatt, was thankfully short, and Wynter was happy for that. Not that she intended to change her mind. She just wondered if he would live up to her expectations after all these years.

The bellhop greeted them upon arrival and immediately opened Wynter's door.

"Thank you," she responded, alighting from the vehicle. Riley was quickly by her side, wrapping his arm around her waist and leading her toward the entrance. Wynter didn't notice much about the lobby, only saw polished marble floors and a teakwood front desk as she allowed Riley to lead her to the private elevator for the residences. He had one of the penthouses on the top floor. Wynter wasn't surprised he would pick a place with all the bells and whistles, such as a twenty-four-hour concierge. He had done quite well for himself since leaving San Antonio.

Once inside the elevator, where they were the only occupants, Wynter stared at Riley. She didn't move, let alone breathe, as he stepped closer, never taking his eyes off her. He reached out and lightly stroked her cheek. "You're not exactly who I thought you were, Wynter."

"I suppose you thought I'd become a shrinking flower? Well, that's not me—it's just been a trying week."

"I can only imagine, but we're going to put that behind us." He tilted her head back with his hand, exposing her throat. Then he leaned down and kissed her neck.

"Yes, let's," Wynter managed to eke out. A gasp of surrender escaped her lips when he trailed hot kisses down her neck. His caresses were smooth and silky, and when he nipped at a particularly sensitive spot, her breathing became labored and her body shivered with delight.

"You've handled it very well," he whispered, his lips brushing her ear.

Wynter sucked in a deep breath. "Th-thank you." She

refused to swoon in his arms, but damn it if her legs didn't feel weak. "But let's not talk about that anymore. In fact, let's not talk at all."

She grasped Riley by his suit lapel and pulled his mouth down on hers. He felt like heaven, and a sigh escaped her lips. Riley took over and kissed her deeply. His tongue slipped inside her mouth and teased and tangoed with hers in an intimate dance she couldn't wait to finish. Instead, the doors of the elevator pinged. They separated, and Wynter stepped out into a stunning penthouse with floor-to-ceiling panoramic views of downtown San Antonio.

"Riley, this is amazing." Wynter walked over to take in the sights.

"Nothing is more amazing than you." His eyes were dark and flared with heated desire. "But I should remind you that I don't do commitment, Wynter."

She spun around to face him. "Well, that's good, because I'm not looking for one."

If Riley thought she was looking for a ring on her finger, she wasn't. Wynter had seen what marriage and commitment looked like with her parents and Corey. None of whom had a union she was looking to imitate. Wynter considered herself much like her aunt, a free spirit with a zeal for life and new adventures. She wasn't looking to settle down with a man, not even her dream guy, Riley Davis.

"Can I tell you that's hella sexy?" Riley responded and started removing his suit jacket and toeing off his shoes. "You're a woman after my own heart."

Wynter smiled. Riley, apparently, was done waiting and didn't want any further delays for the main event, and neither did she. She suspected they weren't going to make it to the bedroom. She'd never been an exhibitionist, but she kind of liked that all of San Antonio was laid out in front of them. Reaching behind her, Wynter pulled the zipper down on the rhinestone dress and let it pool around her feet.

She watched as Riley began stripping with speed rather than any sort of finesse. Wynter couldn't wait to see his sculpted body. And when he took off his shirt, revealing his broad and chiseled chest, she wasn't disappointed. She was transfixed as he removed his trousers. Her eyes moved to the hair that arrowed lower beneath the waistband of his boxer shorts, which revealed the jutting proof of his arousal. She let out a pent-up breath when his shorts hit the floor. "You are beautiful."

"I should be saying that to you."

She smiled and went to shove her panties down her legs, but Riley had covered the space between them quickly. He placed his hands over hers. "Please, let me."

He removed her panties and undid the clasp of her bra, releasing her full breasts. Immediately, her nipples turned turgid when they were exposed to air and his heated gaze. He cupped them in his palms, swiping his thumb back and forth across the hard peaks. When he leaned forward to take one of her nipples between his teeth and tongue, she let out a satisfied moan of pleasure.

Riley grinned. "You like that?"

"I do."

"Good. Because I'm about to give you a whole lot more." Then his mouth was closing around the nipple. He sucked it deep into his mouth, and Wynter threw back her head as shock waves of need coursed through her body. He feasted on the one breast and then transferred his attention to its twin, drawing it into the hot cavern of his mouth.

When he was finished with that torment, he began working his way down her body until he came to her abdomen. He dropped to his knees so he could run a probing finger between the tight curls at the apex of her thighs. A sob escaped Wynter's lips at being touched where she wanted him most. And Riley didn't stop there; he pressed his finger inside, pushing upward until he hit that spot full of nerve endings.

"Ah…!" Wynter cried out.

He slipped another finger inside, sliding them both in and out in an erotic dance. Wynter sobbed his name when the first exquisite spasms of pleasure overtook her body. "Riley!"

She flew apart and her legs gave out, but Riley held her tight, pushing her toward the floor-to-ceiling windows to keep her upright. Sensations were still coursing through her and Wynter didn't think she could withstand any more, but Riley wasn't done. He changed course and began to minister to her with his mouth, slowly licking her damp folds.

When he flicked his tongue against her tight bud, Wynter could once again feel herself teetering on the edge of that magical place. When he began to suckle, her eyelids fluttered closed and uncontrollable shudders began to rack her body as a second climax struck. This man understood a woman's body and knew how to give intense pleasure.

He reached beside them on the floor and pulled protection out his wallet and dealt with it. Then he surged to his feet. Her entire body was trembling with the need to feel him inside her. She tilted her head and they were back to kissing again, the hunger between them passionate and unabated. When she felt the solid ridge of his penis against her moist opening, she instinctively knew to part her legs as he thrust deep.

"Yes!" Wynter cried out because the sensation of having Riley inside her was so perfect. He pushed her thighs apart and set a hard and fast rhythm as he took her against the window. He pistoned into her body with unfettered passion, and their bodies grew slick with sweat as their breaths commingled in pleasure of the acutest kind.

"Oh!" Nothing had prepared her for this moment. All Wynter could do was circle one leg around Riley's waist and hold on for the ride as he drove deeper into her. Anyone with binoculars could see them against the window, and it gave her an illicit thrill until a spasm ripped through her. She dug her nails into his shoulders, and Riley clamped his hands on her buttocks.

He thrust hard and deep one final time before groaning out, "Wynter...!"

They stood together with their bodies pressed tight for several minutes in silence as the enormity of what just happened hit them. Wynter thought Riley might immediately retreat, but instead, he lifted her into his arms and carried her into his bedroom.

# Eight

Riley brought Wynter to his bed. He wanted to make love to her properly. That first time in his living room had been a feverish coupling because of the intense attraction they felt. But now, he wanted to take his time. If tonight was all he had, he wanted to show Wynter how much pleasure they could have together.

Wynter wasn't some naive virgin. She returned his touches and kisses and showed him she knew exactly how to make him moan. And when she wanted to be on top, Riley let her without hesitation. She was skilled and brought them both to a culmination that had Riley seeing stars.

Eventually, they took a shower together, but even that turned into a sensuous glide of naked bodies that kept them up until the wee hours of the morning. Afterward, Riley fell into a deep sleep, which was unusual for him. For years, he'd never been able to get more than four or five hours of sleep because, when he was a teenager, he'd been on high alert. He had to make sure his mother was okay and wouldn't harm herself. The pattern stuck when he went to college and then, later, law school. The long nights of studying to stay on top and be the best took their toll until Riley didn't need much sleep to operate.

But last night, he'd slept like a baby because he'd had Wynter's lush body wrapped around him. However, awakening this morning, something was very clear.

He was in bed *alone.*

Sometime in the early morning, after they'd just had the best sex of his life, Wynter had slipped away from his bed. Riley sat upright. *That* had never happened before. He was used to being the one who left, not the other way around.

Riley didn't know whether he should be offended or not. Or perhaps Wynter hadn't been as satisfied as he thought last night? No, he shook his head. Women could fake it, but Wynter hadn't faked a moment of their intimacy. He could tell. She was responsive and very vocal about what she wanted. She hadn't been afraid to take charge of her pleasure or his.

Riley groaned when he thought about the way she'd wriggled down the bed last night to position her head close to his groin. The way she'd run her fingertips over his erect shaft. Her touch had been featherlight, as if she'd reveled in the sensation of having him at her mercy. He'd been enthralled, and rather than fight it, he'd given in. She'd bent her head, taken him in her mouth and sucked him.

Afterward, she'd raised her head and given him a triumphant smile, all the while licking her lips as she caught a drop she must have missed.

It was one of the most erotic experiences of his life. Wynter had moved to the top of the list as the best lover he'd ever had. Although he wished they could have a repeat of the night before, Riley appreciated that Wynter understood the parameters. As a result, she'd left of her own accord, without him having to show her the door like some of his ex-lovers.

At least he would always have the memory of their one hot night. But, in the back of his mind, Riley would always wonder what might have happened if she had stayed.

Wynter stood under the shower taps and let the water pour down on her. The last few days had been crazy. The funeral, the reading of the will, her date with Riley—which had culminated in the most amazing sex of her life! Sweet Jesus! She'd had no idea how in over her head she truly could be until she tangled with a man like Riley Davis. But she gave as good as she got, Wynter thought with a smile.

She'd brought the man to his knees when she pleasured him with her mouth, but that was only after he damn near had her speaking in tongues after the way he'd taken her up against the glass, later, in his bed and, again, in the shower. Riley had an insatiable appetite, which matched hers. Wynter never knew her sex drive was so high until Riley had brought it out in her. She guessed it took a special person to tap into that side, and Riley was that person.

Wynter didn't have any more illusions about how good they would be together, because Riley had shattered them. It was why she had exited before Riley could wake. She wasn't interested in the awkward morning-after talk. Riley had been up-front about his feelings on commitment. He wasn't looking to settle down. And neither was she. Her family life was abysmal, and it had only gotten worse since her return to San Antonio.

She was hoping things might improve today. Her mother had invited her over to the house to talk. Turning off the taps, Wynter dried off and dressed. She didn't know what to expect, given how they'd left things after the reading of the will, but Wynter was willing to listen. If her mother knew her in the slightest, she had to know Wynter would share her aunt's wealth. She certainly wouldn't spend all the money in one lifetime. Wynter just wanted to live comfortably and be able to travel and write.

Looking through her suitcase, Wynter found what she was looking for in a pair of slacks and a belted snake-print tunic top. An hour later, she was pulling her BMW into the driveway of the Barrington estate. Agnes had been kind enough to drive her car over and Wynter had driven her home. She hadn't gotten around to turning it in yet. She had barely exited the vehicle when her mother opened the front door. That was unusual. Her mother didn't deign to answer her own door. Wynter's Spidey sense went on alert.

"Wynter." Her mother kissed her cheek when she approached as if they hadn't not spoken in the three days since the funeral.

"Mother," Wynter said, "is everything all right?"

"Yes," her mother responded, closing the door. "I'm so glad you came. I'm hoping we can put all this unpleasantness behind us."

"I would like that." Wynter didn't know what was going on, but followed her mother to the great room, where sunlight peeked out from the two-story windows. But then, after glancing around the room, Wynter noticed they weren't alone. A strange man was with them. "I'm sorry, did I come at a bad time? If you're finishing up business, I can come back later."

"No, no," her mother said, motioning her forward. "I wanted you to meet Reginald Price, my lawyer."

"Lawyer?"

"Yes, he thought it best we sit down and hash things out like family before we get the courts involved."

Wynter's eyes narrowed. "And you thought bringing your *lawyer* to a family meeting was prudent?"

"Don't take that tone with me, Wynter Barrington."

"Then don't blindside me," Wynter responded. "I came here in good faith, thinking you wanted to repair the rift in our family, but instead, you brought your attorney? Why? To browbeat me into signing over my inheritance?"

"Of course not," her mother huffed. "But surely you see this is too much for you to take on. My sister's estate is vast, and you don't even stay in one place longer than a week. How are you going to handle her business affairs?"

Wynter sighed, inhaling deeply. "I'm capable of handling the household, Mother. I'm not inept, and as for the inheritance, that's what financial advisers are for. I thought you wanted to talk."

"I do."

"And what is your definition of working this out, Mother?" Wynter inquired. "Me giving up everything so you can have your way?"

Melinda jumped up from her seat and began pacing the room "I'm only doing what's best, Wynter. You have no idea how devastated I was to learn my own sister cut me out of her will. I thought we were close. I feel slighted."

"So, this is about revenge?" Wynter asked. "I can see I was misled about this meeting. I think it's best I go."

"Please don't leave, Wynter. I don't want to this to turn into a battle between us. Think of the scandal this could cause if the press got wind of our family squabble."

"Scandal? I'm not the one causing it. You've ambushed me with your attorney when I have no counsel present." Wynter moved toward the doorway.

"Where are you going?"

"I have some pressing business obligations I need to attend to. When I get back, we can discuss it further— when my attorney can be present."

"Wynter, don't you dare walk out that door! We need to resolve this. Just because you're heading out to gallivant all over the world doesn't mean business stays at a standstill."

Wynter shrugged. "You're the executor of the will— it's up to you to keep the estate running. I did speak with Hope and her husband, however, and they've graciously agreed to stay on and take care of the place until I return."

"You're acting like a spoiled and willful child. You

can't run away when you don't like the outcome of a situation."

"I'm a grown woman, Mother, and I don't answer to you," Wynter replied. "Now that you and Daddy have cut me off, I will be looking after myself from now on. Here's my first act of independence." She dropped the keys to the BMW on the table.

"That's your car," her mother stated.

"I know, but until the will is settled, I can't afford it." Wynter was already calling an Uber. When she returned, she'd utilize her aunt's Rolls-Royce until she found a used vehicle she could afford.

"Your behavior shows me more than ever that you're not equipped to handle this responsibility. And you've made my decision clear. I must protect my sister's legacy." Her mother turned to her attorney. "Start the paperwork to contest Helaine's will."

Wynter stared across the room at her mother. How foolish she'd been to think that something had changed—that her mother would finally see how capable she was. For the first time, she was standing on her own two feet and taking care of herself. She had drawn a line in the sand. A line they couldn't come back from.

"Is that really what you want to do?" Wynter asked.

"You give me no choice."

Wynter turned on her heel and walked out. There was nothing more to be said. She had to ready herself for battle.

"Thank you for meeting with me, Ms. Gilbert," Wynter said the following day when she met with the estate attorney Riley had referred her to at her aunt's home.

There had been too great a risk she'd run into Riley if she'd gone to their office.

"Of course. Mr. Davis told me to take good care of you." LaTanya was a beautiful woman with deep chocolate skin. She wore her hair in a ponytail but had on an expensive suit

Hearing Riley's name made a swarm of butterflies take flight in Wynter's belly. She tried her darnedest not to think about the sexy divorce lawyer, but she was having a hard time forgetting the incredible night they'd shared, and it wasn't like she could talk to Shay about it. She had expressly forbidden Wynter from getting involved with her brother.

And yes, she could tell Egypt or one of the other girls, but she didn't want to share the experience with anyone just yet. It was private. Her secret was hers and hers alone. Plus, it wasn't as if it was going to happen again. It was a onetime thing. Or, at least, that was what Wynter told herself. Besides, she had too much on her plate as it was. Growing her business and staying afloat, all the while fighting off her family for control of an inheritance that should be hers.

"What can I do, Ms. Gilbert? My family seems intent on contesting this will."

"They've already taken a big step by filing an injunction against the estate," LaTanya responded.

"When did they do that?"

"Yesterday."

*After* her meeting with her mother. The attorney must have prepared the documents and had them ready to go. The meeting yesterday was merely a stopgap measure before they went full speed ahead with their plans.

"The injunction prevents you from spending any of your aunt's money or selling the estate."

"Can they do that?"

"Temporarily, yes," she replied. "But the burden of proof is on them to show your aunt wasn't of sound mind and body when the will was executed or that you coerced her in some way."

"That was my aunt's home and now mine. I'm not selling. I understand my mother blocking me and my friends from getting the money, but she's preventing the charities and Helaine's staff from getting the money due them." Wynter covered her face with her hands. "This is a nightmare."

"Can you come to an agreement with your family? A settlement, if you will."

"I'd planned on it," Wynter replied, "but then my mother acted as if it was foolish of my aunt to leave me her estate. My aunt thought of me as the daughter she never had."

"Wynter, I'm sorry to distress you. That wasn't my intent. Your family is playing hardball. It's a tactic."

"Which could take months or years, even," Wynter added. "Isn't that right?" She'd done some research on-line and read the horror stories.

"Possibly. We can try to resolve the issue through mediation. If you're open to it."

Wynter needed time. Time to figure out what she wanted to do. Right now, she was too upset and angry to make any decisions. She rose to her feet. "I appreciate you being frank with me, Ms. Gilbert. Let me digest all of this and get back to you."

Wynter watched the woman leave. The last week

had sucked the life out of her. The only bright spot had been the amazing night she'd spent with Riley, but her life was spiraling out of control. All she wanted to do was run. Run far away. And that was exactly what she would do. When she returned, *Wynter's Corner* would be in the black. She would prove to the Barrington family she was a lot stronger and more resourceful than they gave her credit for.

# Nine

*Two months later*

"Ms. Barrington, we're so excited to have you here at the Aspen Summit ski resort," the resort's general manager, Karen Holt, stated when Wynter arrived in Aspen late that afternoon. It was a brisk thirty degrees out, but the snow made the entire city look like a winter wonderland. "We've loved the stories you've done for other hotel brands and thought you could do the same for us."

"I'm excited to be here," Wynter replied as the manager showed her around the resort.

She'd arrived in Colorado Springs after spending the past couple of months in Europe, with a stint in Thailand. When she'd left San Antonio, she'd needed to get away, not just from the contentious relationship with her family, but from her mixed emotions after the incredible night she'd shared with Riley.

She had never felt the kind of raw passion she felt when they'd been together. She hadn't recognized the woman she'd become in Riley's arms. She'd been so shattered by the experience, she'd left before dawn. For him, it might have just been sex, but for her, it had been a transformative experience. A few days later, she was on a flight, one of many over the past couple of months. And now she was at this beautiful ski chalet where she would find loads of inspiration and material for *Wynter's Corner*.

"We have lots of amenities," Karen stated. "Our spa is world-renowned, plus we have a salon, a fitness center and heated indoor and outdoor pools with a water slide. We are all about offering a holistic approach to restore and rebalance your health and well-being through a combination of nutrition and natural therapies."

"Sounds wonderful," Wynter replied. The resort was hosting her in exchange for a lifestyle story on her blog and their website.

"Allow me to show you to your room."

A bellboy followed behind them with Wynter's meager luggage, consisting of her usual suitcase and a duffel bag. The resort was known for catering to the rich and famous. She wouldn't be surprised if she saw a well-known actor or singer walking the luxuriously appointed corridors.

Wynter was awestruck when they arrived at the king-size guest room that would be her retreat for the next week. It had a contemporary mountain design and offered stunning views of Aspen Mountain. More impressive was the black stacked-stone fireplace and the limestone en suite bathroom with soaking tub and shower. The walk-in closet easily fit her belongings, and Wynter looked forward to trying out the minibar.

"The terrace is out here." Karen opened French doors to reveal a small table and chairs for two.

"You've thought of everything."

"It's our pleasure. I've already scheduled dinner for you this evening at La Toc, but if you need anything at all, please don't hesitate to ask."

"Thank you so much," Wynter replied.

After she'd tipped the bellboy and closed the door, Wynter flung herself across the massive bed. It was soft and plush, and she sank right in.

She needed this.

She'd been going nonstop for months, because she was determined to do everything in her power to make sure *Wynter's Corner* was a success. And she was well on her way. Within weeks of leaving San Antonio, Wynter's efforts at connecting with famous female basketball star Jasmine Butler who loved to travel paid off. They had partnered and shown how to live like rockstars at a St. Bart's resort and consequently, *Wynter's Corner* had blown up. Jasmine had an enormous following, all of whom wanted to know everything about Wynter. Consequently, her subscribers list on her social media skyrocketed. Suddenly, advertisers and sponsors were calling her to show off their travel destinations including the Aspen Summit resort. Now her blog was in the black.

It came right on time, because she had a lot on her plate. Her mother had doubled down on her efforts to contest the will by having Mr. Price depose all her aunt's staff, as if Wynter had bamboozled her right under their noses. Although her mother had mentioned a scandal, she seemed uncaring of the attention challenging the will could bring their family. Her mother was clearly so upset by Aunt Helaine's actions that she didn't care about negative publicity.

Wynter was thinking about checking in with Hope on her aunt's estate when her cell phone rang. It was Egypt.

"Hey, diva," Egypt said from the other end. "Do you have a time for a Zoom call? You've been pretty remote the last couple of months, and the Gems want to catch up."

"Absolutely. Give me five minutes and I'll send a link."

Soon, Wynter's five friends were staring back at her from her laptop screen and firing away questions like old times. It felt good to be Stateside. After she'd filled them in on the resort, it was Egypt who asked the tough questions.

"Wynter, are you sure you want to keep fighting your family over this inheritance?" Egypt had the phone propped up, and Wynter could see she was shucking corn in her food truck. "It's honestly not worth it. If your family doesn't want us to have the money, it's fine. We'll figure out how to make our businesses work, but we—" she pointed to Asia, Teagan, Shay and Lyric on the call "—don't want the charities or your aunt's estate employees to suffer. Settle."

Wynter snorted. "I'm surprised to hear you, of all people, say that." Months ago, she'd been Wynter's staunchest supporter. "Because settling is the furthest thing from my mind. My parents are doing this to punish me, like I'm some errant child. They are trying to rule me and, consequently, rule you." She pointed toward the laptop camera for emphasis. "I won't allow it. I will agree to my aunt's wishes and nothing more. If *I* choose to give my family a portion of the inheritance, it will be my choice. I will not be bullied or pushed around—not anymore."

"Good for you," Egypt said. "How's the blog?"

"*Wynter's Corner* is gaining followers," Wynter responded. "All because Jasmine Butler and I hung out and the pictures and video went viral."

"The power of social media is amazing, isn't it?" Egypt wondered aloud.

Wynter laughed. "Yes, it is." Being seen with Jasmine had really raised her profile. There had even been a few offers for clothing and makeup.

*Wynter's Corner* was not only out of the red, but last month it made a profit. If this continued, she could keep fighting her parents until the courts decided in her favor. But Wynter knew her friends were eager to start their own businesses. She knew she should call a ceasefire with her parents, but *she* wasn't willing to bend, not this time.

"Will Jasmine be visiting us in Barbados?" Asia asked, folding her arms across her chest.

"No, Asia," Wynter quipped. "It was just a publicity stunt."

Egypt wagged her finger. "Doesn't matter because it worked. And now, you don't need your parents' support. You've got this!"

All the women cheered. "Listen, ladies, I have to go. I arrived at the ski chalet after hours of traveling and I'm ready for a long, hot shower," Wynter said. "I'll talk to you soon." She waved and closed the laptop.

Wynter wished she could tell her friends about Riley, but she knew Shay wouldn't approve of their involvement, though Wynter couldn't call the night they'd shared a relationship. It was a one-night stand, and that was all it could ever be, because Wynter refused to allow herself to get hung up on a commitment-phobe like Riley. She'd rather remain single.

An hour later, after showering and changing into jeans and a thick sweater, Wynter took her laptop with her to the resort's café, where she'd order a drink to warm her up. Weather in Aspen was in the low thirties, and after coming from balmy Thailand, she was chilled to the bone. The café was decorated in a farmhouse style with a modern twist. An exposed ceiling showed the beams and piping overhead, while the floors were vinyl "wood" plank and the countertops were made of stone with wood siding. Wooden tables and chairs were scattered throughout, as were cozy bar nooks, if you were alone and needed to power your device.

Wynter chose one of the empty spots at the bar to park herself and enjoy the authentic coffeehouse vibe. She pulled out her laptop and plugged into the power source. She had to catch up on her wrap-up post about Thailand and her experience there, but first, she needed a drink.

Sliding off the bar, she made her way to the line and ordered a medium chai latte. While she waited, she caught up on replying to some of her Instagram comments. Now that *Wynter's Corner* was doing well and she had more followers, keeping up with her social media took more of her time.

"Large chai latte!"

Wynter heard her drink called and walked to the counter. She was reaching for her drink when her phone pinged with an alert. Wynter was reading the notification when she ran into a wall of solid male. Her instincts went on high alert and her skin prickled with awareness. She recognized that smell, because she had luxuriated in it when they'd gone to bed together.

Riley.

Her mouth became dry, and she swallowed. Of all the places she'd expect to run into him, Aspen, Colorado, wasn't one of them.

Slowly, she raised her gaze and met his dark one. He wore the same look of surprise, and he was holding her cup. "Wynter? What are you doing here?"

Wynter's mouth crooked into a small smile. Well, this was incredibly awkward. She had to face the man she'd gone to bed with, then ghosted. "I'm here to do a piece on the resort for my blog. And you're holding my latte."

"Good to know," he replied, "but this is my drink."

Her brow furrowed. "You like chai lattes?"

He grinned, and Wynter couldn't help it—her stomach flipped. "Yes, I do. And I was here first. I ordered a large."

Wynter immediately let go of the beverage, because she'd asked for a medium. She watched Riley's mouth close around the lid and had to close her eyes. Memories about what exactly Riley could do with his mouth assaulted her. Sweet Jesus, she was in trouble.

Suddenly, the barista was calling out, "Medium chai latte!"

*Thank the Lord.*

Once she took her drink, Wynter stepped away from the counter and walked back to the bar, but Riley was hot on her heels. When she was seated, he took the empty stool beside her. She wasn't sure how to behave in a situation like this. She'd never had a one-night stand before. Usually, if she went to bed with someone, she expected to see them again. Although he was Shay's brother, Wynter hadn't anticipated she would see Riley again so soon.

He seemed equally as flummoxed and stared at her over the lid of his latte.

She had to break the silence. "And you? What are you doing here?"

"I already had a vacation planned before I was hired, so I'm combining relaxation with work. I'm here to woo a potential client," Riley responded. "A reclusive tech billionaire is in the market for a divorce attorney. I'm hoping to convince him I'm the right fit."

"I'm surprised you would need to *try*," Wynter replied.

Riley's reputation was stellar on the East Coast, as well as in San Antonio. Although she'd told herself not to, since she left, she'd kept up with Riley, who'd made a big splash since his arrival.

Riley laughed. "I've had wealthy clients before, but this one is going to be tricky."

"How so?" Wynter asked, taking a sip of her drink.

"Because custody is involved," Riley explained. "And although I have an excellent track record for my clients, I typically try to avoid cases where children are involved, but it's not always possible."

"Why?"

Riley hungrily ate up the sight of Wynter, with her wavy hair and gorgeous light brown eyes. To say he was thrown was an understatement. And not just by her question, but by Wynter herself. When they ran into each other, his breath had jammed into his lungs and his heart had hammered in his chest. He'd felt winded, as if he'd been punched in the gut, because all he could think about was the softness beneath the snug sweater and denim jeans she wore. She was a burst of heat on a cold winter's day.

Two months ago, they'd shared the most memorable night of his life. Although he tried to bury himself in work, he'd been unable to forget. He felt a tug of lust deep in his belly that told him the attraction toward his sister's best friend hadn't ended after one night. It was still there. Brighter and hotter than ever.

"Are you going to answer me?" Wynter asked. Her question forced Riley to blink several times and reset—before he hauled her over his shoulder and took her back to his room, where he could reacquaint himself with all her lush curves.

"Of course," he replied. He put his latte on the bar. "The kids are put in the middle during a divorce. Sometimes having to choose between one parent and another. When I do cases with children, I make damn sure kids are left with a parent who can love and support them."

"Because you know from personal experience?" Wynter asked.

He nodded. He didn't usually talk about his parents' divorce, but it was different with Wynter because she was Shay's friend. "Yes. It wasn't easy. My father wanted to split our time between him and Mom fifty-fifty, but she was adamant we stay with her full-time. Shay and I felt like we were in a tug-of-war. And seeing how hard the separation was on my mom, we chose to stay with her. My father was disappointed, and I think it's why he chose to push us away when he remarried."

"He punished you for choosing your mother?" Wynter inquired.

Riley nodded. "But we had to stay with her. Mom was fragile. If we had gone, I'm not sure if she would be with us today." He'd never told anyone that, but with Wynter, he felt he could be open about the hardships he and Shay had endured as teenagers.

"But your mother is doing better now."

Riley nodded. "It wasn't an easy road to get here, Wynter. She needed the right treatment and care, but yes, now that we've found the right combination, she's well."

"I'm so happy for you and Shay." Wynter touched his arm, and Riley's nostrils flared as he caught a hint of her sweet perfume. It dragged him back to that night at his penthouse when Wynter had aroused him like no other woman.

Everything stilled as he looked deep into her eyes. The world narrowed to nothing but the two of them, and Riley battled to control the craving he had to tunnel his hands through her hair and bring her closer to him right there in the middle of the café. So he talked about work.

"It's not easy for me to take on clients with children, but this case is different. The wife doesn't really want the kid. She's using the child as a poker chip in a power game with her husband. She's holding custody over his head so she can get what she wants."

Wynter's hand flew to her chest. "That's horrible."

"Exactly. It's why I want to help. When my partners told me about it, I knew I needed to put aside my qualms and step in, but the client has refused to meet."

"Then you'll have to change his mind," Wynter said. "And if anyone can, you can."

Riley cocked his head to one side. "I never knew you had such faith in me." When he locked his gaze on her, Wynter licked her lips. He wished he could taste her one more time.

Wynter broke their gaze and looked over at her laptop. "Well, I need to get back to work."

"Of course—I'm sorry to have kept you."

"You didn't."

"How long are you staying?" Riley inquired. "Perhaps we can have dinner? That's if your boyfriend doesn't mind."

Her brows knitted together. "Boyfriend?"

"I can't assume a woman as beautiful as you is still single, especially considering how popular you've been lately."

Wynter laughed. "Sounds like someone has been following me."

Riley chuckled. She wasn't wrong. After they'd connected in San Antonio, he'd subscribed to *Wynter's Cor-*

*ner* and followed her on her social media accounts. "Not closely, but if you were putting it out there for public consumption, can't blame a guy for looking." Yes, that sounded better. He didn't sound like he'd been stalking her or was some lovesick puppy.

"If you must know, there's no one."

"That's good. Because that means there's no reason we can't have dinner."

"Do you really think that's wise after...?" Her voice drifted off. It was the first time during their conversation they were acknowledging what had occurred between them months ago.

"C'mon. We're friends, right?" Riley asked. "Surely we can enjoy a meal together without ripping each other's clothes off?"

"Speak for yourself," Wynter murmured under her breath, but Riley heard her.

"Well, I'm going to be down at the bar around seven," Riley said, getting up from the bar stool. "If you're there, great. If not, the message has been received loud and clear." Grabbing his latte, he tipped his head to her and left the café. Riley didn't look behind him, even though he wanted to. She wanted to pretend they were immune to each other, but he knew otherwise.

Tonight he would find out if Wynter was willing to take a risk and acknowledge that what they shared was far from over. In fact, it had only just begun.

# Ten

As he drove to Derek Webster's twenty-thousand-square-foot ski chalet on Aspen Mountain, Riley's mind should have been focused on his upcoming meeting. The tech giant had finally consented to giving him an audience so Riley could pitch himself as the best attorney to help fend off Derek's soon-to-be ex-wife from walking away with half his assets. Texas being a community-property state, his spouse wouldn't get half his company, because he had owned the business prior to their marriage, but the ski chalet, among several other properties, had been acquired during the marriage and thus was jointly owned.

Instead, he was thinking about his run-in with Wynter. He hadn't thought he'd seen her again, at least not for a while, and certainly not in Colorado on a business trip. The relationship between them had changed; she wasn't just a friend of his sister—she was the woman he wanted. And he wanted her in the worst way. One night hadn't been enough to satiate his needs. If Wynter chose to come to the bar tonight, he would ask for the whole week, the entirety of his stay. He didn't know how long she was going to be here; all Riley knew was that he wanted her in his bed. And he suspected she wanted the same thing.

When he arrived at the stunning chalet, even Riley had to admit he was impressed with the four-story single-family home. He'd read the reports and knew it was worth upwards of seventy-five million and was one of the bones of contention in the Webster divorce. His wife wanted it, and Derek openly refused to give up the oasis that came with a full spa, indoor and outdoor pool and Jacuzzi, a movie theater, and a bowling alley.

Closing the door on the Jeep he had rented for his stay, Riley walked up the path to the front door. He hadn't bothered getting dressed in his finest suit, because Derek wasn't likely to care about that. He was informal, preferring jeans and a T-shirt to a designer suit. More importantly, Derek could afford thousands of Riley's suits several times over; he would instead impress the man with his knowledge and legal acumen.

He rang the doorbell and, to his surprise, Derek answered himself. The man had a mop of dark hair, piercing blue eyes and wore a hoodie and jeans.

"Riley, c'mon in." Derek motioned him inside. "I was watching March Madness. Are you into basketball?"

"Yes, I am," Riley said, closing the door. "Though

I'm more into the NBA, I'm happy to watch a college game."

"Good, then you can join me for a beer," Derek said and turned on his heel. Riley had no choice but to follow him. He walked across the custom Italian-porcelain tile floor, past the Lalique crystal chandelier, to the elevator. They took it to the top floor, which housed the kitchen and an open-concept living and dining room, as well as a recreation room. The game was playing on a large television. Riley recognized the other gentleman in the room as Derek's right-hand man, Craig Abbott.

Riley walked toward him. "Craig," he said, shaking the slender blond man's hand. "Good to see you again. I appreciate you setting this meeting up."

"You're welcome," Craig responded. "We heard what you were able to do for David Goldman, and I suggested to Derek that he should at least meet with you."

"What are you drinking?" Derek asked from the hidden refrigerator that was seamlessly integrated into the kitchen's white walls.

"I'll have a Miller Lite if you have it."

Derek handed Riley a bottle and joined him and Craig on the couch to watch the game. Riley didn't know when they would talk business, and he wouldn't push it. When Derek was ready, Riley would pitch exactly how he intended to save the tech giant billions.

That time didn't come for nearly two hours. Instead, the three men enjoyed beers and trash-talked until the game finally ended and Derek wanted to talk shop.

"Tell me why I should hire you," Derek asked, using the remote to turn off the television. "You don't usually take cases where custody is involved."

Derek had done his research. Riley was not surprised. "No, I don't, but I'm very familiar with your case. I'm sure you've seen my stats. I've won my last ten cases."

"None involving children," Derek replied.

"True, but I'm one of the best divorce attorneys out there. Losing is not in my DNA. I will go to battle for you, Derek, and make sure your wife abides by the prenuptial agreement she signed."

Derek snorted. "That woman is a lying, cheating barracuda. She will do anything, say anything, to get her way. I want custody of my son, and my wife knows this. Knows there's nothing I won't do, including give her more than the prenup says is required."

"What does she want?"

"This house. Shares in my business, which, as you know, is not community property."

"Yes, I'm aware. Mrs. Webster is devious, but I've beaten her lawyer in court many times and I will again if you give me the chance to represent you."

"And you'll win me custody of my son?"

"I will do my very best to ensure your son is with a loving parent, and that's you."

"You intrigue me, Riley," Derek replied, "but I'm meeting with several attorneys while I'm here. I'll have to get back to you."

"Of course." Riley rose to his feet. He didn't want to overstay his welcome. "I appreciate the beers and the game. Would you be interested in joining me tomorrow to go snowmobiling? Fresh snow is expected later this evening—it would make for a great ride. You could get to know me from an old family friend who knows my character."

"Not a bad idea. Tell Craig and he'll arrange everything."

"Sure thing," Riley said. On his way to the car, he wondered what else he could do to show Derek he was the man for the job. It was true, he didn't usually take cases with children, because he hated seeing families split apart and the effects it had on the children. He knew this firsthand. His parents' divorce had torn him and Shay asunder. Riley wasn't sure he could handle dealing with the fallout day in and day out. But based on a private investigator's report, Riley suspected emotional abuse by Nina Webster, and now he felt compelled to intervene. He couldn't let her go unchecked. He just hoped this case wouldn't unearth his own demons, which had been dead and buried for years.

"Wynter, so glad I was finally able to catch up with you," LaTanya stated later that evening. Wynter had been working on her blog all afternoon and had just returned to her room. "You've been a hard woman to find."

"I'm sorry, Ms. Gilbert. I've been traveling and am now Stateside. Do you have an update for me?"

"I do, but I'm afraid it's not what you wanted to hear."

Wynter sighed. Although the answer wasn't unexpected, she'd been hoping her mother would let the matter go. She supposed that was wishful thinking.

"They've asked the judge to have an independent audit of your aunt's financials completed."

"Why?"

"My guess is they want to see if there any anomalies or irregularities, such as large outlays of cash to you or anyone else. This is all to support their case that your aunt was not of sound mind and body when she executed the will."

"That's ludicrous!"

"Are you sure you don't want to settle? Or do you want to stay the course?"

Wynter was silent on the other end. Over the past couple of months, she'd given the situation a lot of thought. Every time she thought about giving in, she remembered that her aunt had wanted her to have her home and the means to enjoy whatever lifestyle she wanted, nomadic or otherwise.

"Are you there?" LaTanya asked.

"Stay the course."

After the call, Wynter looked at the time. It was 6:00 p.m. and getting close to when Riley said he would be at the bar. Wynter's mind told her to stay in the room, but another voice told her to go downstairs and meet Riley for that drink.

Months ago, she'd justified the one-night stand by telling herself they were just scratching an itch and she would be able to move on afterward. She'd been wrong. She hadn't been able to so much as look at another man, much less be intimate with anyone, since Riley. He'd left an inedible mark on her. It was as if he'd branded her *his*. Her self-preservation instinct told Wynter to run, but that was what she always did when life got too difficult. Staying and seeing if the spark she'd still felt in the coffee shop was real or imagined would be a test for her.

She could either leave what they shared that one night as a fulfillment of her teenage crush, or she could take a risk, as Riley had suggested, and face the music on what was going on between them. Wynter was scared. She feared she could fall for Riley, a self-professed serial dater. He wasn't interested in the long-term, just the right now.

Even if Wynter wasn't looking for a ring and a white picket fence at the moment, she did want a family *someday*. If she got too close to Riley, it was quite possible he could penetrate the shell she'd erected around her to protect herself and she'd want more. The only way she'd dealt with not belonging in her family was not letting anyone in, except maybe her girls. Her best friends were like her sisters. They were the closest thing she had to a family, but they weren't a lover. Riley had the power to undo her defenses with one look or caress of his lips.

She should definitely run.

But instead, somehow her feet led her to the bar. The lounge offered a wood-burning fireplace, a 165-inch television and lots of comfy and plush sofas and chairs paired with small cocktail tables. Then there was the bar itself, with high-backed chairs that easily sat twenty. Four chandeliers that looked like art installations hung over the bar. There was even an outdoor patio that gave an uninterrupted view of the mountain. It was exactly the type of place Wynter's parents would frequent, but usually not her. She preferred a more casual setting. However, she was determined to show Riley she could handle whatever he dished out.

She found him standing near the only empty bar

stool in the place. He smiled as she approached. "I'm glad you came."

"Did you think I wouldn't?" she challenged.

"No. You don't strike me as a coward," Riley said and pulled out the empty stool.

"Thank you," she said when he slid it underneath her.

"What can I get you to drink?"

Wynter glanced around. "I feel like in a place like this, I need an old-fashioned."

He chuckled while signaling the bartender over. After ordering her drink, he turned his full attention to Wynter, and she sucked a deep breath as his clean yet spicy scent reached her nose.

"What have you been up to the last couple of months?" Riley asked. "Were you able to come to an agreement with your family?"

Wynter shook her head. "Afraid not. They seem determined to paint me as the bad guy, but I refuse to accept the role. They're contesting the will, and I get that they're upset with me and don't want my friends to inherit anything, but they are preventing good charities from getting funding and allowing my aunt's employees the compensation due them."

"I'm sorry to hear that," Riley said. "I hoped things would be different by now."

"You mean, you didn't ask Shay about me?" Wynter lifted a brow.

Riley reached for the bottle of Miller Lite he was drinking and took a swig. "And risk her wanting to know why I was asking?" He shook his head. "No, thank you. My sister wasn't happy during your aunt's funeral when she thought we were spending too much time together."

"Why is she so dead set against it?"

Riley regarded her. "She thinks I'll hurt you."

"Will you?"

"Not intentionally," Riley responded, looking her in the eye. "Listen. I like you, Wynter, and I thought one night together would be enough to quench the hunger I have for you. After we were together, I realized it wasn't, but you were already gone."

His words, like a silken caress, wrapped around Wynter's fast-beating heart. She shouldn't still feel like this. They had only been together one night, yet it seemed as if that invisible cord she'd felt before kept bringing him back into her orbit.

"I thought it was better than having an awkward morning after," Wynter replied. Picking up the old-fashioned the bartender had set down, she took a sip.

Riley's dark eyes were lit like two flames, and she could feel her nipples puckering underneath her shirt in response.

"I haven't stopped wanting you since that night."

The atmosphere suddenly became charged, and Wynter had to remind herself to breathe. Hazarding a glance at him, she said, "Weren't you the one who said you didn't do commitments?"

Riley nodded. "That's true, and I'm not looking for marriage and happily-ever-after. I see the dark side of marriage every day, Wynter, after the vows and the re-criminations. I don't know if I can believe in the institution. I've seen too much. I know how devastating it can be for both parties."

"It's a jaded view of the world, Riley. Not every marriage fails."

"The divorce rate in the US is steadily increasing. It's 2.7 to every thousand. The major cause is infidelity, because we're not meant to be with one person."

"Are you saying if you made that commitment, you would be unfaithful?"

"Hell, no!" Riley's emphatic response was rather shocking, considering his view on marriage. "I'm never marrying, so that wouldn't happen, but if I did, I would take my vows seriously. People give up too easily. Marriage is about a choice. You have to choose that person every day, even when the going gets tough."

"That's very powerful."

"I guess. I never thought I'd have a heated discussion about marriage with a woman I can't wait to get alone."

"Well, you're going to have wait a little longer, because I'm starved," Wynter responded. After the topic of conversation and the heated stares Riley had given her earlier, she needed to cool things off between them until she could figure out her next move. Though she feared she was a lost cause.

She wanted Riley.

Could she resist his advances?

And did she really want to?

Riley was doing his best not to let his mind drift and think about how good it could be with Wynter, but it was difficult when she smiled at him across the dinner table. It made him think of her soft moans when he'd been buried deep inside her.

Wynter was doing a good job of distracting him with other topics. He learned she was a basketball fan like him and had loved the San Antonio Spurs in their heyday. She didn't like food that was too mushy in texture. He couldn't believe it when she said she didn't like soft-serve ice cream and preferred hand-scooped ice cream because it was hard. The suggestive comment made her blush and made Riley want to lean over and give her the openmouthed kiss he was longing to, but instead, they continued talking well into the evening.

Riley discovered Wynter wasn't a fan of classical music and instead liked old-school rhythm and blues groups. They had a heated discussion on Boyz II Men versus Jodeci. He was a Jodeci and Silk fan himself and doggedly defended that "Forever My Lady" and "Feenin" were some of the best songs of the '90s, while Wynter preferred sweet love songs such as "End of the Road" and "I'll Make Love to You."

"You say I'm a romantic," Riley said, "but those are baby-making songs."

Wynter laughed, and the sound was rich, firing his body on all cylinders. Flames licked over his skin, and Riley had to shift in his seat. To change the subject, he asked Wynter if she wanted to accompany him on the snowmobiling excursion. Having Wynter and Derek together might lighten the mood so the billionaire didn't think him too pushy.

"I would love to come," Wynter said.

"Great!" Riley responded.

When the waiter came and asked if they wanted dessert, they simultaneously responded with an emphatic "No."

"I really enjoyed dinner and the conversation," Wynter said after Riley took care of the bill and they rose from their seats.

"So did I." But he also wanted to enjoy *her*.

Anticipation zinged in his veins when he placed his hand on the small of her back and led her out of the restaurant.

They made it to the bank of elevators, and Riley sensed Wynter's uncertainty. He pressed the up indicator, and they waited in silence. Riley would never push her into doing something she wasn't ready for. If tonight wasn't right, he'd wait. He was going to be here a week, or however long it took to win Derek's business.

When the elevator pinged and the doors opened, they entered the cab. Wynter pressed the fifth-floor button. It took all Riley's willpower not to take Wynter in his arms, but he stayed on his side of the cab. Several moments later, they arrived on Wynter's floor. She didn't say anything as Riley walked beside her until they arrived at her door.

Suddenly, she turned to face him. "I..."

Riley looked down at Wynter with her sexy, wavy hair and bee-stung lips. A hungry possessiveness came over him, but it would have to wait for another time. He placed his thumb on her lips. "Nothing has to happen tonight, Wynter. I'll see you tomorrow." He turned to leave, but Wynter clutched his arm. Her pupils were dilated and her lips parted.

Riley felt his soul sing, and as he tilted his head, he told himself, *Just one kiss*.

And then he took her mouth.

* * *

One touch of Riley's lips on hers was like a flame to dry kindling, because Wynter swore her entire body ignited. Hot and firm, his mouth teased hers, brushing softly at first and drawing out the pleasure. She restlessly moved against him, urging him on. He deepened the kiss, and a moan broke through the heated silence of the corridor as his tongue boldly caressed hers.

Wynter was drowning in sensation, so when he angled his head for better access, she gave it to him. She wrapped her arms around his neck, and his fingers surged into her hair as the kiss took on a frenzied feel. Their bodies were plastered together, hip to hip, chest to chest, and their mouths were fused, their tongues gliding together as one. It was every bit as glorious as she remembered.

When his hips sought the cradle of her thighs and Wynter felt the evidence of his erection against her, liquid heat began to form between her legs as her body readied itself for his possession. That was when it hit Wynter—they were in the hall, where anyone could see them.

With a hoarse cry, she pushed against the solid muscle of his chest until he released her.

He frowned, a dazed look in his eyes. "Wynter?"

"I'm sorry. That shouldn't have happened." She tucked her hair behind her ear.

"As kisses went, it was pretty damn incredible," he responded, but he backed up to give her some space.

"I need to think about this," Wynter said, even though her body ached for more. "Before we start something."

"I understand, and I won't push. When you're ready, you'll have to make the first move. Good night." Riley pressed his palm to her cheek, and then he was striding down the hall and making Wynter wish she'd called him back to finish what they'd started.

But she was right to stop. She needed to be sure she could take having a full-blown affair with Riley. Because, although he made her feel wanted, it was only sex to him. She couldn't make the mistake of thinking the attraction between them was anything more than physical. The moment she did, she would be opening herself up to heartbreak.

# Eleven

Riley didn't know how he'd walked away from Wynter last night. He only knew he'd had to. He was trying to be a decent guy, but it wasn't easy. The way she responded to him told him she wasn't unaffected by him, but he understood her reluctance. He didn't believe in love and marriage and the whole bit. He'd discovered how much love cost. Had lived in the shadow and pain of that love. It was why he enjoyed the company of women *casually*.

Although she hadn't said it, Riley wondered if Wynter wanted marriage and babies. Maybe not right this second, but at some point. And he would never be able to give her that. He was too jaded. But he could give her this amazing week. They would enjoy each other's company, and when it was over, they would move on with their lives.

Those were his thoughts as he walked down to the ski resort. For the day's activities, he wore a puffer jacket, a turtleneck and ski pants, and underneath were wicking long johns and a long-sleeved top to ensure he was warm yet comfortable. He was stopping for a coffee when he heard his name called.

He smiled when Wynter approached, wearing a similar ensemble of ski jacket and pants and a crew top. "Good morning," she said brightly.

"Good morning. How did you sleep?" he replied. Was her sleep as miserable as his? She'd occupied his thoughts for much of the night. Thinking about having Wynter in his bed had made him hard, and he'd finally gotten up in the middle of the night and taken a cold shower.

"I slept wonderfully."

*Liar.*

"Great, then you'll be ready for a day of snowmobiling. I hope you don't mind, but I invited the client I'm wooing along."

She shook her head. "Of course not. And although I've never been snowmobiling, it's going to make a great article for my blog."

"Good. C'mon, let's get that coffee."

After they ordered their coffees, they made their way to the lobby, where Derek and Craig were already waiting for them. Derek was in appropriate ski clothing and ski boots, but Craig wasn't.

"Great day for a ride, Riley!" Derek stated.

"Indeed," Riley responded. "Derek Webster, I'd like you to meet Wynter Barrington."

"Nice to meet you," Wynter replied.

"Likewise," Derek said, nodding.

"Craig, are you not coming with us?" Riley asked.

"Oh, no. While you guys zip through the forest, I'm having a spa day. You guys enjoy." Craig waved them off and walked away.

Derek scoffed. "Why did I give him the day off? I should have made him join us."

"And what fun would that be, having a Debbie Downer along?" Wynter asked. "That just means there will be more fun for the three of us."

Derek glanced at Riley. "I like her. She's a keeper."

"I think so." Riley looked at Wynter, and he loved that she still blushed. "C'mon, follow me."

Riley had a private limo waiting outside that would take them to a ranch that specialized in snowmobiling. "Nice touch, Riley," Derek said when they climbed into the warm vehicle. "What else do you have in store for us?"

"I would love to know the answer to that, too," Wynter said.

"We're going to tour Maroon Creek Valley and have lunch at a private cabin," Riley replied.

"You thought of everything," Wynter said, winking. "I'm impressed."

Riley wasn't just wooing Derek; he was using all the tricks up his sleeve in the hopes that, by the end of the day, Wynter would be willing to move from a one-night stand to a full-blown affair.

Wynter was glad Derek was in the limo. It made it easier to keep her distance from Riley. After that kiss outside her hotel room door, Wynter's resolve was crumbling. She had wanted him to come inside, but was glad her sanity returned before she dived headfirst into a physical relationship with Riley.

Shay hadn't been wrong when she said Riley had the power to hurt her, but the other side of the coin was that Wynter enjoyed being with him, laughing with him, talking with him. And, yes, making love with him. Riley was an amazing lover, and Wynter wanted to experience the pleasure she'd found in his arms again. But was it worth the risk?

It didn't help that Riley was looking across the limo at her as if she were a double scoop of double-fudge ice cream. His heated gaze made Wynter squirm in her seat, until she eventually looked out the window to avoid his stare.

When they made it to the ranch, Wynter was the first out of the limo and eager for their lesson, but first they had to sign a release waiver and listen to the safety briefing. Once the lesson was over and they were outfitted with helmets, it was time to ride.

"Are you sure you can drive one of these on your own?" Riley inquired, glancing down at her.

"Of course," Wynter snapped. "And in case you didn't notice, the minimum age is eighteen."

"Don't give the lady a hard time, Davis," Derek said. "She's got this." He gave Wynter a fist bump.

"Thank you," Wynter responded.

They followed their tour guide, Matt, down to the snowmobiles. Derek would follow the instructor, then Wynter and Riley would bring up the rear.

"Are you guys ready?" Riley asked once they'd all hopped on their snowmobiles.

Wynter gave a thumbs-up. "Let's rumble!"

Soon, their snowmobiles were barreling through exquisite mountain scenery. Wynter couldn't believe this was her life. It was so far removed from how she lived in San Antonio and what her parents wanted for her. She felt completely free.

The two-hour tour was brisk and concluded with them stopping at a beautiful rustic cabin, tucked in the mountains, for a late lunch. As soon as they arrived, the chef on-site poured hot cocoa to warm them up. Derek was busy chatting up the tour guide, which left Wynter and Riley alone with their mugs to look at the view from the large bay windows.

"It's beautiful here," Wynter said, sipping the hot drink. The cabin had a spectacular view of the Maroon Bells.

She felt Riley behind her as he came closer. "Yes, it is, but I honestly only have eyes for you," he whispered in her ear.

"Riley," she said, glancing behind her. "Don't."

"Don't what?"

"Put on the charm," Wynter muttered. "You already sampled the goods."

He laughed heartily behind her. "True, but I would like a repeat performance." He circled his arm around her waist and brought her closer into his body. It felt good having him hold her, and it made Wynter want to set aside her misgivings. They were supposed to have only had one night. If they changed course and became lovers again, it was a risk—mostly to her heart.

She spun around until they were facing each other.

Wynter looked up into Riley's scorching gaze and knew she already had her answer.

*Yes, yes, yes.*

She would throw caution to the wind for a chance to be in his arms again.

"Here's the lovebirds." Derek approached, and Wynter stepped backward. "Oh, don't separate now because of me. I appreciate you letting me join you. Today was a lot of fun. I think my son would love something like this."

"I hope you don't mind me saying so, but that's why you should hire Riley. He thinks outside the box," Wynter said, putting down her empty mug.

"Let's talk over lunch," Riley interjected. "The food is ready."

The chef was motioning them over to a circular wooden table, where he'd laid out a delicious three-course meal. The appetizer was charred squash with Asian pear soup, and the main attraction was a braised veal loin with cipollini onions and fingerling potatoes, accompanied by crispy brussels sprouts. They all dug in, but soon Derek got a call and stepped away from the table.

"Can I give you some advice on how to convince Derek to hire you?" Wynter asked.

"I'm all ears."

"Over the appetizer, you were reiterating your stats and why Jamison, Charles and Davis is one of the best firms in the country, but you haven't made this personal to you."

"What do you mean?"

"I think if you share your past and tell Derek how

your parents' divorce affected you, it might give him some perspective on why this case is important to you."

"I don't talk about my personal life with clients."

"I get that," Wynter replied, "and you don't have to share everything, but help him understand…" Her voice trailed off when Derek returned.

"Help me understand what?" Derek inquired.

"Why he's the right man for the job," Wynter stated. She inclined her head toward Riley. His hesitant look told her he wasn't sure of her plan, but Wynter knew it was the right thing to do. Every attorney was telling Derek what they thought he wanted to hear, but showing a touch of vulnerability and humility could go a long way to helping him see why Riley was different.

Riley leaned back in his chair and regarded Wynter. Being with her today had been fun. He liked her carefree spirit and willingness to try new things. She was kind and honest and had hit it off with Derek instantly. When they stopped for photos earlier, he'd seen the other man's spark of interest in Wynter. Riley supposed that was why he'd made his presence known once they got to the cabin, so Derek would know she was taken.

Derek was being good-natured about it, but he also hadn't given Riley a decision yet. Maybe Wynter was right—if he opened up about himself, Derek might find him more relatable. Not that he was in a rush to seal the deal, because the longer he was here, the more time he got to spend with Wynter.

"I've talked about my stats," Riley began, "told you why I'm one of the best divorce attorneys out there, but what I haven't told you is that I've been in your son's shoes."

"Pardon?" Hearing his son mentioned made Derek sit up straight.

"My sister and I were pawns in my parents' divorce," Riley stated. "I know firsthand what it's like to be shuttled back and forth between parents. To have them pit us against the other. To feel powerless because you didn't get a say in who you want to be with. If you hire me, Derek, I will fight for your son and his best interests. I'll ensure custody is given to the caring and stable parent who loves him. And that's you."

"You're very impassioned, Riley," Derek replied. "I appreciate you sharing your story with me. Unfortunately, I have to head back to my chalet. I have an important business meeting to attend."

"Completely understand," Riley said.

Derek turned to Wynter. "You, my dear, are enchanting." He kissed Wynter's hand.

Suddenly, the roar of a helicopter could be heard overhead.

"That's my ride!" Derek smirked. "I called my pilot. Enjoy dessert. And you—" he pointed at Riley "—I'll be talking to soon."

Several moments later, he was rushing out the door.

"Oh, my God! Do all billionaires have a helicopter at the ready?" Wynter inquired.

"Apparently, yes," Riley replied as they watched the helicopter take off. "And where did the chef and the tour guide head off to?" he asked and walked into the kitchen. He found a note on the counter.

*The cabin has been rented for you both to share for the remainder of the day, courtesy of Mr. Webster. The chef has left the dessert on the counter, and there's meals in the fridge. I will be back for you in the morning.*
*Matt*

"What does it say?" Wynter asked, leaning over Riley's arm.

Riley couldn't help but chuckle. That sly devil Webster had just ensured he would have uninterrupted time with Wynter. If they were alone, there was no way she could deny the attraction between them.

"Did Derek really strand us here without our guide?" Wynter asked, folding her arms across her chest.

Riley turned around and leaned against the counter. "It appears that way."

Her eyes narrowed. "Did you arrange all this? Was this your way of convincing me to reignite our affair?"

Riley's brows furrowed. "Wynter, I don't have to resort to these sorts of games to get a woman in my bed."

"Is that so?"

"Yes, because they usually don't need convincing."

Wynter scoffed. "Maybe I do."

Riley shook his head. "You know what you want. Don't be scared. Take what you want."

He hoped she would. Their eyes locked from across the room. He dared her to forget logic and go with her instincts. He wanted to splay his hands all over her body and remind her how good it was between them, but she had to want it, too. The lust Riley felt for Wynter overpowered him. It had since the moment he laid eyes on her at the River Walk.

Would she give them what they both wanted?

Wynter huffed out a breath.

No man had ever gotten under her skin like Riley. Everything within Wynter urged her to let go, because the need she saw in Riley's eyes mirrored the primal pull she felt inside her own body. But he didn't make a move to meet her halfway. He'd told her last night that *she* would have to come to him.

No time for second thoughts. Wynter stepped toward him and planted her palm on his chest. She felt the solid muscle underneath, and his drumming heart.

Riley's dark eyes were hooded as they looked down on her, hard. "Are you sure? Because if you're not, I'll call someone to come get us."

Her response was to lean her body into his and circle her arms around his neck. Then she brushed her lips gently over his as if she were relearning the taste and texture of his mouth. Her body craved this man, and Wynter felt she might fly apart just from kissing. He tasted so damn good, and his lips fit hers perfectly.

Wynter tossed out logic and went with the moment.

With need.

With longing.

They stripped off each other's clothes along the way to what she presumed was the bedroom. Once there, their mouths and hands feverishly explored each other's bodies until she moaned for him. When he joined them as one, she felt full, complete.

For a moment, they both stopped breathing, and

Wynter wanted to stay like this forever, but the need was inevitable. Their bodies rocked together as one, and Wynter reveled in the ecstasy she could only find with Riley. A tidal wave crashed over them both. Riley collapsed on top of her, and Wynter held him to her as if she never wanted to let him go.

# Twelve

Riley brushed Wynter's damp curls away from her face as she lay snuggled against his chest. The incredible sexual intimacy they'd shared blew his mind. He'd never felt it with another woman. In his casual relationships with others, it had been about physical gratification, but with Wynter it felt different. He didn't recognize the emotion; he knew it was special. He loved Wynter's uninhibited responses and that she freely gave of herself during lovemaking.

He was thoroughly bewitched.

He would, however, have to make it clear that the affair would last only while they were here in Aspen. Once they returned to their separate lives, they would resume their friendship. Riley hoped that was possible. The women in his life usually understood the rules of engagement when it came to dating him, but Wynter was different. They had grown up together. He *knew* her, and not just in the biblical sense. He would have to tread carefully, because he didn't want her to get confused or hurt. He cared about her. He wanted her to be okay afterward.

He must have voiced his concern aloud, because her eyes fluttered open and she looked him square in the eye. "Do I not seem okay?"

"I want to be sure you have no regrets," Riley replied. "This was rather...*spontaneous*. And I want you to know that I in no way planned for this to happen, but I'm not sorry it did, either."

"Neither am I." Wynter caressed his chest with her warm palm. When she touched him, his heart rate sped up, and his erection swelled to life.

"Then what do you say to a round two?"

Rather than answer, she curled an arm around his neck and brought his mouth down to hers. Riley sank into her arms and into the unfettered passion between them.

Much later, after having made love for much of the evening, they surfaced for food. It was dark outside, and Riley found a few candles to make the setting feel romantic and special. Wynter wore Riley's long-sleeved shirt, while he'd slipped on his boxer briefs. They found the makings of dinner in the fridge: Wagyu burgers, a container labeled Truffle Mac 'n' Cheese, and a platter of petit fours.

Riley fired up the stovetop grill and cooked the beef to perfection while Wynter heated up the pasta and sourced plates and cutlery. Once they had plates in hand, Riley opened up a bottle of pinot noir from the wine cellar they'd found next to the walk-in pantry and poured them each a glass. The chef hadn't lied; they definitely wouldn't go hungry.

"This mac 'n' cheese is to die for." Wynter closed her eyes and sighed after she'd indulged in a couple of bites. When she opened them, she found Riley's scorching gaze on her. "What?"

"If you keep making those little moans," Riley said, picking up his burger, "I'll have you back in the bedroom and flat on your back before you can finish your meal. I'm already having a hard enough time concentrating with you wearing next to nothing."

Wynter blushed and glanced down at the shirt, which stopped above her knee. She wasn't wearing anything underneath. They'd been so eager for one another when they'd made love, their clothes had gone flying, so she couldn't find her panties. It wasn't as if Riley was clothed, either. His chest was bare, and all Wynter wanted to do was press her mouth to his pecs and run her tongue down the hard planes of his stomach. She wanted to taste his skin. And those thighs? The man must hit the gym pretty hard, because they were like granite.

She had to remind herself that, although she was living in the moment, life was short and her time with Riley was fleeting. It wouldn't be long before they were back to their normal lives and this would all be a memory.

"You're frowning," Riley stated.

Wynter blinked. "Am I?"

"Yes. And I think I know why, which is why I propose we spend the rest of the week together," Riley responded. "I don't know how long you're staying in Aspen, but I have to be here until the end of the week. I was hoping…" His eyes grew dark with desire.

Wynter picked up where he left off. "We continue sleeping together while you're here?" she offered. She didn't know if she should be excited or offended. Excited, because the sex between them was off the charts and she couldn't wait to wash, rinse and repeat. Or offended that he thought she was so *easy*.

He looked a bit stunned at her directness, but answered, "Yes. Do you have a problem with that? You could even move into my suite."

She didn't. After Aspen, she had a month before the girls' trip to Barbados. She would go home to San Antonio and see if she could finally make peace with her family.

"If you have other plans…" Riley started, but Wynter shook her head.

"It's not that." Wynter sighed. "It's just difficult being estranged from my family." Yet somehow, looking across the candlelit table at Riley, a man she'd known and crushed on since she was a teenager, Wynter felt she could share her truth. "I've never felt like I belonged."

"I can't understand what it's like to feel that way in your own family, but when I went to Princeton, most of the kids there were legacy. Their parents and their grandparents attended, and here I was, this Black kid from San Antonio on scholarship. I didn't feel like I was a good enough, like I belonged."

"What did you do?"

"I pushed myself to be the best. When I began to rise to the top of my class, my confidence grew. Suddenly, everyone wanted to talk to me and be my friend, especially the ladies."

"Is that when you decided to only pursue casual relationships?"

Riley shook his head. "I've always known I'd never marry. I saw the destruction it caused when you loved someone and they left you. I never wanted to feel that way."

"So you don't stay," Wynter surmised. "You leave them first."

Riley chuckled wryly. "I think this conversation has gotten way too deep."

Wynter didn't think their talk had gone deep enough. Riley was the first man she'd felt comfortable sharing the bad stuff in her life with, but he was hesitant to reveal more about himself.

"You haven't told me about any of your relationships," Riley said, changing the subject.

Wynter shrugged. "I've dated."

"Has there ever been anyone special?" Riley inquired. "A long-term, committed relationship?"

*No, because they weren't you*, Wynter thought. She supposed she had built him up in her mind as her ideal man so much that no other man ever came close. She shook her head. "Not really."

"Then we're alike," Riley responded. "We keep people at a distance."

"You may prefer an arm's-length relationship, but not me," Wynter replied.

"No? Then why haven't you found the one? Are you

too picky? Are you one of those women with a laundry list that has to be checked off before you'll deign to get serious?"

"Not at all. I'm just selective. *When* I settle down with that someone special, it'll be because they're the one person I can't live without."

"You're living in a fantasy if you think one person can ever measure up or be all that you need. It's foolish to love. I've seen how it can hurt, especially when someone lies or leaves."

"It doesn't always have to end up like that. If you both grow together and want the same things out of life, then no one gets hurt. Love is the reward."

"You're an optimist, Wynter. I'm a divorce attorney, remember. I've seen just how bad it can get."

"You're saying that because you're hurt," she murmured under her breath. Wynter wasn't sure if Riley heard her, but if he did, he chose to ignore it.

Instead, he said, "You never answered my question."

"You mean about whether I'd like continue our affair while in Aspen?"

"I do believe that's the question on the table."

"Well, Counselor," Wynter said, turning toward him at the bar, "I think I need some convincing."

The intense look Riley gave Wynter sent shivers through her, and she could scarcely breathe. His gaze raked over her in his shirt until her nipples tightened into hard points. Riley noticed, because his eyes became laser focused on her breasts. Her breathing became rapid, and her breasts began to rise and fall as she thought about what Riley could do to them.

When he rose to his feet, anticipation prickled her

skin and lust slammed into her. She never suspected Riley would throw her over his shoulder and stride to the bedroom, where he promptly tossed her on the bed before joining her.

Soon, they were creating their own rhythm, until sensations began to build inside her and all Wynter could see was this one pleasurable moment. And when it arrived, breaking free from its constraints, she let out a keening cry, while Riley roared out his climax.

White-hot pleasure licked through her veins, and Wynter felt completely satiated, because she was with Riley—the man she was falling in love with.

As promised, the next morning, Matt, their tour guide, arrived to take them back to the ranch by snowmobile.

Riley and Wynter were ready, having already donned their ski outfits after a sublime morning session in the shower that started with Riley washing every inch of Wynter's body and ended with her plastered against the tile wall as he plunged deep inside her body. Riley was thankful he'd kept a pack of condoms in his wallet. If he and Wynter were going to spend the rest of the week together, he would need an entire box.

No one made him feel the way Wynter did.

Making love with her, he discovered things about his body and hers. He was totally attuned to her, and his response, as a result, was heightened. This week was going to be one helluva week to remember, especially because he'd have Wynter in his bed every night.

They arrived back at the resort and parted ways, vowing to get together later that evening once Wynter had a chance to pack. She indicated she would be trying one of the resort's yoga classes and the spa, so she could write about the experience while Riley caught up on work. Although this was technically a vacation, Riley didn't know how to press the off switch. He was getting ready for opening arguments on one of his cases that couldn't be settled while working on Derek's contract. He was certain the tech giant was going to hire him. He was the best, after all.

Once he was back in his suite, Riley immediately turned on his phone and found he had missed several messages. He'd turned off his phone while he was at the cabin and forgotten to turn it back on. There were a couple from his assistant, Ronda, about an urgent matter on one of his cases, and then there was Shay. He thought about calling his sister back and then thought better of it. What if Wynter told Shay she was staying at the same resort? His sister could have a million questions, and he wasn't in the mood to answer them.

He went for work instead, contacting his assistant and working straight through lunch until his stomach growled and demanded satisfaction. Grabbing a quick sandwich gave him time for his mind to drift to the silkiness of Wynter's skin and the waviness of her hair. Or her amazing scent, which drove him wild.

Since they'd agreed to dinner, Riley had his assistant arrange for them to eat at the chef's table. Chef François Du Bois had a six-course tasting menu that was divine. Afterward, Riley planned on taking Wynter to bed and ravishing her until they were spent. He didn't understand the hold Wynter had on him and why he couldn't get enough of her, but by the end of the week, the chemistry would burn itself out. It always did.

Wynter was impressed by the resort. After yoga, the staff had arranged for her to get a facial, manicure and pedicure at the spa, and when she mentioned she was having dinner later, Karen, the resort manager, treated her to getting her hair and makeup done at the salon. By the time she left, Wynter felt hydrated, plucked and made into the best version of herself. She would need it for her evening tonight.

Yesterday's rendezvous with Riley had certainly not been something she had planned. Wynter had assumed their one night a couple of months ago was all she would ever have to remember Riley by, but instead, he'd shown up at the resort where she was working and somehow still found her desirable. It seemed too good to be true.

But it was real, because she had the soreness between her thighs to prove it. They were very active in the bedroom. Riley was an exciting and inventive lover, the best she'd ever had. Deep down, though, Wynter knew her feelings for him ran deeper than lust alone. She genuinely liked him, possibly loved him. Had she ever stopped?

They could talk for hours, as they had last night by candlelight. The topic didn't matter, because Riley was knowledgeable on politics, art, music and films. It made Wynter want to delve deeper to the man underneath.

Riley, however, wanted to keep her at arm's length and restrict their relationship to this week in Aspen. In her head, Wynter understood. He and Shay had endured a lot during their childhood, but he was throwing the baby out with the bathwater. He wasn't allowing himself to feel anything because he was afraid of the effect it might have on him—that he might turn into his mother and never recover if he lost that love.

Instead, he was willing to go through life never experiencing the emotion. Wynter wanted him to see that sometimes it was worth taking the risk. Being on her own the past couple of months felt like teetering on the edge of the abyss with no idea of what lay below, but she'd done it. She'd had to. Her parents had given her no choice. Why didn't they believe in her? Why were they so willing to think the worst? Wynter couldn't understand it.

On an impulse, after returning to her room, Wynter dialed her mother's number. It rang several times before her mother's curt voice came on the line. "Wynter, I'm surprised to hear from you. I thought all our conversations had to be handled through our lawyers."

"They don't have to be," Wynter responded.

"I'm glad to hear that," her mother said. "When we hadn't heard from you, I was beginning to think you wanted all of my sister's wealth for yourself."

"That's not true." Wynter was hurt by her mother even thinking that, making her feel the need to lash out. "I didn't ask for any of this. You're the one contesting the will and making me the villain in this scenario."

Her mother sighed wearily. "What was I supposed to think, Wynter? You refused to even consider a settlement."

"Because that isn't what Aunt Helaine wanted," Wynter replied hotly. "I'm honoring her wishes. Why can't you see that? Or are you blinded by the money?

Heaven forbid, Wynter, the screwup in the family, should have what's rightfully hers by law."

"It's not fair!" her mother yelled into the phone.

Wynter was taken aback. Melinda Barrington rarely raised her voice, but Wynter also wasn't about to be her whipping girl. All her life, she'd wanted to be seen by her parents, but she had always fallen short. This time, she wasn't backing down. "I'm sorry you feel that way, Mother. I'm sorry to have bothered you."

"Wynter, wait!" her mother whispered. "I'm sorry I yelled, okay? I'm just out of sorts about all of this."

"You think I'm any better? I hate this." Although they'd never been close, at least they'd always been civil and sociable.

"Come home, Wynter," her mother said. "You haven't been home in months."

"I haven't been home because I've been working on my business. *Wynter's Corner* is finally making a profit."

"Oh, my God, Wynter, I had no idea. I'm very proud of you."

"You are?" That was a surprise. Wynter wasn't used to receiving any praise from her parents. Usually they were telling her what she did wrong or what she needed to improve on.

"Yes, I am. Please come home so we can talk in person," her mother said.

"I'll give it some thought."

"All right. Take care of yourself, Wynter." And then the line went dead. There were never any *I love you*s with her parents. They didn't do warm and fuzzy. That was for other people.

Wynter expected it. When she'd fallen down and bruised her knee or someone at private school pushed her down and ripped her uniform, there hadn't been anyone to wipe away the tears and kiss the boo-boos. Eventually, Wynter had hardened her heart and acted like she didn't need love and affection, but there was another part of her that had always yearned to be loved.

Embarking on a casual affair with Riley ensured she would never get that love from him, but Wynter couldn't walk away. He did it for her in every way imaginable. Could she navigate the murky waters of this affair and come out unscathed? Or was she making the biggest mistake of her life, getting involved with a man who would never give her the love she so desperately craved?

# Thirteen

"This is way too much," Wynter said several days later when Riley ordered nearly everything on the room service menu, from ahi tuna, calamari and goat cheese croquettes to a wild mushroom flatbread, so they could have a picnic on the floor of the suite.

Since she'd moved into his suite, they'd established an easy rhythm. While Riley attended to his cases, she worked on her assignment for the resort. During their free time, they'd gone skiing, snow tubing and dogsledding, which was exhilarating. Tonight, however, they weren't in the mood to dress up in bulky gear. Instead, she was in her flannel pajamas, while Riley wore a T-shirt and sweats.

She loved how comfortable they were, hanging out together and just talking. Tonight, their conversation had segued into their college experiences.

"Leaving home was a breath of fresh air," Riley said. "It was the first time I was free to have fun without fear of getting a call about my mother. When I was in high school, I would be called away from lacrosse practice or a party because my mom was freaking out."

"I'm so sorry. I know how hard that was," Wynter said. She'd seen how hard it was on Shay.

"When I arrived at Princeton, all I did was keep my head in the books, but then my roommate reminded me that I was young. There would be plenty of time to figure out who I was going to be, and I should be a little bit naughty. I frequented the frat parties on campus, and soon I was a hit with the ladies."

"Is that when you became a ladies' man?"

"Not initially. I didn't have as much experience going into college, but I more than made up for lost time," Riley said, grinning.

"I just bet you did. Tell me your craziest college story," Wynter said. "I know you have to have one."

Riley's eyes were alight with mischief. "If I tell mine, you'll tell yours?"

Wynter grinned and nodded.

"One night, we were all sitting around the dorm with not much else to do and started playing a drinking game. I got dared to streak across the dorm."

"Did you do it?"

Riley laughed. "I did and narrowly escaped the RA. Needless to say, I never did that again. How about you? What's your story?"

"Well, I'm not proud of it," Wynter began, "but I was jealous of a friend of mine going out with a guy she knew I wanted to date. When they arrived at a friend's birthday party, words were exchanged, and, well, I sort of threw the birthday cake in her face."

"Oh, my God!" Riley roared with laughter. "No, you didn't."

Wynter nodded. "Oh, yes, I did. It was hilarious in the moment, but then she proceeded to chase me across the campus in the dead of winter. When she caught up to me, she pushed me into the snow, and an epic snowball fight ensued."

Riley held his stomach as he laughed. "Your story is way funnier."

"Needless to say, neither one of us ended up with the guy. He thought we were too immature."

"Thanks for sharing."

"Oh, I made plenty of boneheaded decisions in my youth, more so to get my parents' attention than anything else."

"Have you always had an acrimonious relationship with them?" Riley inquired, nibbling on a piece of the flatbread.

Wynter shook her head. "Quite the opposite. They've never seemed to care what I did so long as I wasn't embarrassing them. Now, the shoe is on the other foot, because they're choosing to air our dirty laundry in public. I don't understand why. It's not like my mother isn't wealthy in her own right. Why is she so insistent on fighting for Aunt Helaine's estate? The only thing I can think of is she doesn't want *me* to have it."

"You really believe that?"

"There's no way else to think, Riley," Wynter responded. "If this were Corey, she wouldn't be putting up a fuss. I know every parent has a favorite, and I'm clearly not it."

"Well, you're my favorite person right now," Riley said and, to her surprise and utter delight, pulled her into his arms. But instead of giving her an earth-shattering kiss like he always did, he held her tight like he had that first night on the River Walk. It was exactly what she needed.

She'd been right in her decision to live in the moment and take advantage of being with Riley, because it might never come again. After the compliment, he had added "right now," meaning their time would soon come to an end. Wynter refused to be one of those clingy women who hung on. When the time came, she would be the first to walk away.

"Riley, thank you for coming back up the mountain," Derek stated when Riley arrived at his home the next morning. Derek brought him to the dining room table on the upper floor of his villa. "Please have a seat."

Riley sat down and waited. He had done everything in his power to win Derek's business, including talk about his past, but the billionaire had been a hard nut to crack.

"Of course." Riley took off his overcoat and slung it over the back of his chair. He was done pursuing Derek. It had been nearly a week, and Riley had to get back to San Antonio. If Derek didn't know Riley was the best man for the job by now, Riley would have to accept it.

"I was hoping we could finally settle some business," Derek said. "I appreciate your patience in allowing me to conclude all my interviews with the other attorneys."

"Have you made a decision?"

"Yes," Derek responded. His blue eyes were trained on Riley. "I'd like you to represent me."

Riley clapped his hands. "Excellent news. Derek, you won't be disappointed. I've already taken the liberty of drafting the contract." He pulled the document from his briefcase and slid it across the table.

"I'll have my attorneys look this over. Honestly, I knew the day you told me about your parents' divorce that you were the right man, but the businessman in me had to be sure and check all the boxes," Derek responded. "Seeing you this week with the lovely Wynter made it clear that you have a good head on your shoulders."

"I do," Riley said. "And I've already prepared a draft of a temporary order to get you visitation rights, since your wife has taken custody of your son."

"You're not wasting any time," Derek said.

"No, I'm not. I want to win, but I also want to see you with your son," Riley replied. Hearing Wynter's story last night was tough. She had wanted her parents' affection so desperately. Even now, at twenty-seven, she still wanted it. He would do everything in his power to prevent Derek's son from experiencing that sort of heartbreak.

Wynter was falling hard for Riley. Since she had discovered him in the café, they'd spent every day together, in and out of bed. And now, on their last day, Riley had told Wynter he had something special planned after he met with Derek. There were times throughout the week she had found Riley watching her with such an intensity, her blood had sizzled. Wynter hoped the affair they were having might morph into something more, but he'd been mum so far.

Yesterday, when they'd walked to the shops in town hand in hand, Riley had picked up gifts for his mother and Shay, which was to be expected. However, he'd surprised Wynter when he chose a beautiful necklace in the shape of a butterfly for *her*. It was a simple piece, and Wynter didn't wear much jewelry because she traveled, but when he'd seen her admiring it, he'd insisted on purchasing it. Told her it matched her perfectly, just like she matched him.

Wynter had felt dazzled. She'd never received gifts like that from other men. Maybe because none of them had been the right one, the one for her, like Riley was. She wanted to believe they could *be* more, *have* more someday, but Riley was so adamant he didn't believe in love or marriage. With each passing day, her hopes had begun to crumble. Was she a fool for staying with him?

All these musings kept replaying through her brain, so when Egypt called, Wynter spilled her guts. She'd kept their affair to herself the entire time because it had been their secret, but now she *had* to confide in someone or she'd burst. Thankfully, Riley was out of the suite for a meeting with Derek, so she had it all to herself.

"Hey, girlfriend," Egypt said cheerfully on the other end of the line. "What's it like hanging out with the rich and famous in Aspen?"

"Wonderful, crazy and romantic."

"I don't understand. I get the wonderful and crazy part if the hotel is pampering you and giving you anything and everything to ensure you write a great puff piece, but where does the romance come in?"

"It's Riley," Wynter blurted out. "We've been having a clandestine affair the entire time I've been here, and now I think I might be in love with him, but he doesn't want love and marriage and I don't know what to do."

"Whoa! Wait a minute," Egypt said, interrupting her tirade. "You and Shay's brother have been getting busy? Say it ain't so."

"It's so. Very so," Wynter replied. "Riley is an amazing lover. Hell, he's the best I've ever had, and I knew I shouldn't have gotten involved with him. I should have let San Antonio be a onetime thing, but then we ran into each other again and—"

"Wait just a minute," Egypt interjected. "Are you telling me you and Riley slept together in San Antonio? Like, a few months ago, after your aunt's funeral, and I'm just now hearing about this?"

"Oh, Lord!" Wynter covered her eyes and hung her head low as if Egypt could see her. "Don't be mad."

"Mad? Girl, I'm not mad if you want to get your swerve on, but at least spill the tea to your best friend!"

Wynter chuckled. "I'm sorry. It was supposed to be a onetime thing, but then I saw him here in Aspen. And, well…"

"The panties dropped."

"Honey, yes!" Wynter laughed, which released some of her tension. "I can't resist the man. When I'm with him, I feel complete, like I've found my person."

"But he doesn't feel the same way?"

"That's the thing, Egypt. I think he does. I don't

think he could make love to me the way he does otherwise."

"Sometimes sex is just sex to men, sweetheart," Egypt responded. "They don't get emotionally attached like we do."

Wynter sighed. "That's what I'm afraid of. What if I'm all in and he's got one foot out the door?"

"I'm worried. I don't want you to get hurt."

"It's a little late for that. I guess that's why Shay warned me away from him," Wynter replied. "But I didn't listen."

"She doesn't know?"

"No."

"I wouldn't tell her," Egypt said. "No sense in causing a rift between siblings if you guys don't last beyond this week. If the connection turns into a relationship, then you'll have to let Shay know."

"Egypt...what do I do next?"

"Wynter, you know I have always kept it real with you. I don't know how to do anything else. Talk to Riley. Tell him how you really feel."

"And if he doesn't feel the same?"

"Then you'll know one way or the other, but at least you won't be guessing and tying yourself in knots."

Wynter knew Egypt was right, but it didn't make it any easier to listen to her advice. "Thank you, girlfriend." She stared down at the phone. Was she prepared for the end of their love affair?

No.

But she needed to know how Riley felt. Or was she deluding herself into thinking he could feel anything more for her other than affection, caring and lust? Wynter sighed. She would never know unless she went out on a limb and revealed her true feelings, but she was afraid of his response.

She was used to her family's indifference, used to being invisible, but with Riley she felt seen, heard and *wanted*. But if he verbalized that he didn't feel the same way, it would be a crushing blow to her self-esteem, and it might take Wynter years to recover. She would weigh her options, and only if the situation presented itself would she tell Riley she loved him.

"Is everything all right?" Shay inquired later when Riley returned to the suite for his special day with Wynter. She was in the other room putting a bag together, so Riley had FaceTimed Shay to do a well-being check on their mother. That was when she told him Eliza was not only happy but thriving with her new male companion. They were at brunch and going to the movies later.

Riley could hardly believe the change in his mother. It was so profound, he struggled to understand how she could go from the despondent creature ravaged by heartbreak to the smiling and alluring woman he'd seen over the past months. It was as if the last two decades hadn't happened, and she was the mother he remembered from his youth. It was unsettling, but he'd felt hopeful about his mom's situation for the first time in years.

"Everything is fine," Riley said to Shay, who peered back at him from the screen. "Why you do you ask?"

"I dunno, there's something different about you." Shay tilted her head this way and that, as if she were trying to figure out a puzzle. "You seem lighter, less weighed down. If I'm honest, you seem relaxed."

"Do I normally not seem that relaxed?"

Shay shook her head. "Absolutely not. I'm afraid you always have a stiff upper lip, brother, as if you've perpetually tasted something sour."

Riley couldn't resist laughing at her comment. "Thanks a lot, Shay."

"Hey." She shrugged. "What can I say? I know your career can be stressful, dealing with the demise of marriages and families."

"It can be," Riley admitted, but he tried his best not to show it. Apparently, though, he wasn't doing a very good job of hiding it. This week, however, he did feel lighter, freer, as if anything was possible. And he knew why.

Wynter.

She had been a ray of sunshine in his life. They held engaging conversations, and when she wasn't around, he wanted to be with her. Yesterday, when an adorable necklace caught her eye in a store, he'd had to buy it just to see her face light up. Riley would have bought Wynter a more expensive trinket, as he usually did for his women when the end of their affair was near. This time, however, he'd bought the gift because he wanted to. Even though she'd been born into wealth, Wynter didn't care that the necklace wasn't expensive or extravagant, because she was a down-to-earth, kind woman.

"Riley!" Shay was calling his name.

"Yes?"

"Did you hear a word I've said?"

He blinked and racked his brain, but the past couple of minutes had been a blur. He'd been fantasizing about Wynter.

"I'm sorry, no," Riley replied. "I missed what you said."

"It's not like you to daydream." Shay's eyes narrowed on his iPad screen. "Now I'm definitely on alert. Are you seeing someone?"

"Why would you ask that?" Riley said, his voice rising.

"Well, are you?"

"Wherever would I find the time?" Riley responded. "I'm here in Aspen for vacation and partly for work, to catch that big client I told you about. I don't have time to date."

"If you say so."

"I do."

"Well, then you should be dating," Shay responded. "I don't want you to end up alone. Although I may have made a mistake with Kevin, I still believe in love and want to find the one."

"You're an optimist, Shay, you always have been. I'm just not wired that way." Although spending time with Wynter had given him pause. If there was ever a woman who might make him want to change his mind, it was Wynter, but Riley didn't believe in all the love mumbo jumbo. So he shook it off. "I'm glad Mom is doing well, and I'll call you when I'm back in town." He hung up before his sister could wax poetic about the joys of matrimony. His feelings on the subject hadn't changed, but he was beginning to see the merits of having a permanent lover.

Wynter was incredible, and they shared a connection. Riley had enjoyed himself more in the past week than he had in years. It didn't have to end here in Aspen. Rather, they could see each other whenever Wynter was in San Antonio. Once the will was validated and Wynter gained her inheritance, she would need to check in on the estate often. Perhaps she would consider extending their rendezvous indefinitely?

There was only one way to find out.

He was going to have to ask her.

# Fourteen

"You've really outdone yourself," Wynter said, sinking down in the hot springs after a refreshing cold-plunge dip. He had brought her to this resort outside Aspen that had over twenty-five steamy geothermal pools. The therapeutic waters were known for their healing benefits due to the minerals found inside.

"I'm glad you like it," Riley responded. "We're both leaving tomorrow, and I wanted to do something special for an exceptional woman."

"It's very thoughtful," Wynter replied. Even though Riley tried to act cold and distant, he cared about those closest to him and did thoughtful things for them. It's one of the reasons she admired him, aside from the fact that he was gorgeous, smart and funny.

She and Riley had already tested out each pool, because each one had a different temperature and feel.

Some were for socializing, while others were quiet and spacious. They opted for a quiet one so they could have privacy.

When they'd arrived, they'd changed in the locker rooms, and after they'd emerged, Riley had been naked from the waist up, with a smattering of black hair on his powerfully broad chest, which tapered into a path below to his swim shorts. Wynter had wanted to eat him up as if he were chocolate ganache.

Riley had caught her tongue wagging, and his eyes, which sometimes were darker and deeper than the night, had connected with hers. Even though she'd seen him naked tons of times, he still had an effect on her. He was gorgeous, with a masculine assurance all his own, and Wynter was absolutely head over heels for him— but he had no idea.

She resolved to keep her feelings tucked away until the right moment. It didn't happen that afternoon, when they enjoyed the pools, or when they had a relaxing aromatherapy couple's massage, or at dinner when they returned to the ski resort. Only later, in Riley's room, when she found champagne and strawberries waiting for them, had Wynter thought about having the talk Egypt had suggested.

Riley had set the stage for a romantic day, and Wynter loved it, but she was also on pins and needles. Should she tell him her feelings? Should she broach the subject of a relationship or commitment? She knew Riley was against it, but she also couldn't help feeling as if the past week might have changed his perspective.

"How would you feel about continuing to see each

other after this trip?" Riley inquired after he poured the champagne and handed her a glass.

Wynter paused midsip. "I hadn't thought about it." She placed the glass on the nightstand and tried, unsuccessfully, to locate the zipper at the back of her strapless dress. She caught her reflection in the mirror and reminded herself to keep away the tears that were threatening to leak out of her eyelids. She didn't want to read too much into his words, but it was hard not to. This man made her weak, and she would have to be strong to tell him how she truly felt.

"Well, give it some thought," Riley said, coming behind her. He swept her hair aside and unfastened the clasp that kept the zipper from moving. Then he slid it down until the dress fell into a pool at her feet. "I don't want this to end." His voice was a gruff rumble as his hands skimmed over her waist and pulled her back against him. She felt him grow large behind her. "We could see each other whenever you're in town."

His other hand went to her breasts. She hadn't needed a bra for the dress, so they were left bare for Riley to knead and caress with his palm.

"So, we would be casual, like your other relationships?" Wynter asked. Desire weakened her, especially when Riley deftly teased her nipple between her fingers and thumb. Heat emanated from his body, and Wynter's breathing became rapid, as if she were running a marathon. When she looked in the mirror and their eyes met, Riley's were glazed with hunger.

Riley tensed behind her, but he didn't stop looking at her. "Don't make it sound like that. We've had a good thing this last week, haven't we?"

Wynter kept her eyes locked on Riley, but she didn't say a word.

"Then say yes."

She watched, transfixed, as he stripped his clothes off behind her and slid on a condom. Even though she was speeding headlong toward disaster, need was ignited inside her.

She uttered the only word she could. "Yes." Then he reached for her panties and pushed them down her legs. She leaned her backside against him and felt the swell of his erection. Reaching around, she grasped him, sliding her fingers up and down his hard length.

Riley's jaw clenched and he groaned, but that didn't stop him from sliding his hands forward, past her stomach, to her nest of dark curls. She sighed when he parted her folds and his fingers stroked that sensitive spot. "Ah-h-h…" she cried out.

Every part of Wynter felt aflame with hunger, because Riley knew exactly how to please her. Her wet inner muscles clenched around his fingers, but then he suddenly moved away.

She moaned. "I need you."

Riley understood and sat on the bed. "Come here," he ordered.

Wynter walked over to him and prepared to ride him, but Riley turned her back around to face the mirror. "Spread your legs."

Wynter wasn't used to him ordering her around in the bedroom, but she didn't mind. She wanted him too much. His large hands splayed around her hips so she could sit astride him with her back to him, her legs on either side of his thighs. She shivered, and her eyes fluttered closed.

"Open your eyes and look at us in the mirror."

Wynter glanced up and was shocked by the wanton woman staring back at her. She was spread wide-open and completely vulnerable. With dazed eyes, she watched Riley's fingers delve inside her slick core. The sensation was so incredible that Wynter rocked against his fingers.

Riley's eyes gleamed with fiery desire, and Wynter could feel molten heat licking along her flesh…her orgasm was coming lightning fast. He must have sensed her need, because he lifted her up so she could sink down onto the thick head of his erection. She shuddered, and he shifted so she could take all of him. When Riley grabbed her thighs and urged her up and down his shaft, blood began pounding through her veins and intense sensations hit Wynter at the friction.

"I'm so close…so damn close," she cried.

"Don't fight it," Riley whispered.

She watched in the mirror as he grazed her neck, pinched her nipples and then slipped a hand between their bodies to the swollen heart of her. The action sent Wynter over the edge into a cataclysmic orgasm that surpassed anything she had enjoyed with Riley so far. Starlight burst behind her eyes, and fireworks exploded inside her head.

"Oh, God. Oh, God!" She panted as Riley pushed hard and insistently into her one final time. She heard his agonized groan as his entire body tightened and he gave himself over to his release.

Wynter's head fell back against his shoulder, her entire body slick from their efforts. Riley bent his head and gave her a deep, searing kiss. Afterward, he eased her away and visited the bathroom, but Wynter's senses were swimming and she was too spent to speak. Instead, she slid underneath the covers in a heap of satiated completion.

Riley sat beside Wynter on the flight back to San Antonio. He'd convinced her to continue their affair past Aspen, and one would think he felt in control, but he didn't. He felt as if he'd lost all perspective.

Last night, the sex with Wynter had seemed even better than before, but it hadn't felt like just sex. He felt as if he'd been reborn after a long winter.

*How was that possible?*

This was supposed to have been an affair for a week, but he hadn't been able to end it, because the electric chemistry between them was unmatched by anyone else.

Each time Wynter surrendered to him, it was genuine, fresh and sweet, and Riley was becoming worried. Fear was creeping in. Fear that this woman could mean more to him than any woman ever had. His instinct for self-preservation was asserting its presence. There was going to be a price to pay for this affair with Wynter. He was addicted to her. Perhaps it was her big brown eyes that seemed to understand so much. Or her warmth and compassion for others.

He never allowed a woman in because the act of doing so was fraught with danger, but Wynter Barrington, damn her, was a puzzle he couldn't solve. He didn't understand her hold on him, when he never allowed women to cross the threshold of making him feel anything. But Wynter was getting perilously close to doing just that. He was starting to forget that this was supposed to be just sex. He'd forgotten that their affair would *end*.

He should let her go now before she got hurt, because she deserved so much more. However, as soon they arrived back in San Antonio, with a limo waiting to take them home, he'd smashed his mouth over hers, demanding more, and Wynter, God help him, gave it right back to him as if she, too, had been stripped down to her raw sexuality.

And so, with a wildness filling his mind and heart, he made love to her for hours.

Wynter returned to her aunt's mansion the next morning. When she stepped inside, she received a warm welcome from Hope, her husband and the rest of the staff. She knew she shouldn't have stayed away so long, but at the time, losing her aunt and facing a battle with her family over the estate had felt like too much. She'd also had to get *Wynter's Corner* into the black, which she'd done. She was super proud of what she'd accomplished in such a short span of time.

If only her love life were such an easy fix. When Riley had suggested they continue their affair in San Antonio, she'd immediately wanted to say no, but then he'd made her come apart so completely in his arms, she hadn't been able to. By avoiding Riley, she would only be hurting herself and going back to self-imposed celibacy. For what? The man she had fallen for wanted to be with her, and despite her qualms, she wasn't prepared to let him go. Maybe Riley was right, that love made you foolish, because Wynter certainly felt he could come to love her. He was halfway there. Or at least she thought so. The way they'd been together last night. So in sync. So in harmony.

It wasn't mindless sex. They'd made love. Afterward, he'd reached for her, hauling her closer to him and snuggling her into his heat. It was as if he'd needed her energy and her strength, and she'd given it. When he'd taken her again, later in the night, savagely driving into her, she hadn't flinched. Instead, she'd wrapped her legs tightly around him and accepted whatever conflict was raging inside him. And when need had morphed into a storm and overtaken them both, they'd looked straight into each other's eyes as if they were the other's safe harbor.

Last night had been a monumental one Wynter doubted she would ever forget.

Wynter did, however, need to speak with her mother and finally settle her aunt's will once and for all. Although she'd traveled the globe for a little over two months to build her business, she'd also needed to get away to heal. But it was time for this feud to come to an end. Rather than wait for an invitation to the Barrington residence, Wynter decided to make a surprise appearance later that week. She and Riley had agreed that both had some pressing matters to attend to and would get together soon. After unpacking her things in the guest room, Wynter took her aunt's car to the Barrington estate.

Agnes was there to greet her as always and led her into the drawing room, where her mother was having tea.

"Wynter." Her mother looked effortless in a sleeve-less floral tunic and white pants. The weather in San Antonio was blazing hot, in the nineties, and Wynter had opted for a simple romper and sandals. "Oh, my God! I can't believe you're here."

"You suggested we talk," Wynter said, taking a seat on the sofa across from her mother, "and I agreed. It's time."

"Would you like some tea?" Her mother sat down across from her and gestured to the teakettle and cups sitting on the settee in front of her.

"I'm not here for tea and crumpets," Wynter said. "What do you want, Mother? What do you want to end this battle?"

"You're so blunt," her mother said. "What crowd are you keeping?"

"Don't sidestep. What will it take to end this so everyone gets the bequests Aunt Helaine wanted them to have?"

Her mother sighed. "You make it sound as if I'm money hungry."

*If the shoe fits*, Wynter thought, but she remained mum. She couldn't stoke the flames. Instead, she stared at her mother expectantly, waiting for a response.

"Well, the Smith family business was sold a number of years ago, so I think it's only fitting the profit should come to me."

"I know you've done an audit of the financials," Wynter said, "so if there's enough to pay all the bequests, I will split half the remainder with you, but I keep the house as gifted to me. Does that sound fair?"

Her mother cocked her head to one side and stared at

Wynter. "Yes, it does. I can live with that. We can put all this unpleasantness behind us. I will contact my attorney and stop the challenge of the will immediately."

"Good." Wynter rose to her feet. They'd come to an agreement, and she could finally move on with her life. She didn't know why it had taken so long, but maybe she could see things more clearly now that she was finally out from under her parents' thumbs. Fighting was not the answer.

"Wynter, wait!" Her mother touched her arm. "Why are you in such a rush to leave? I've missed you."

Wynter snorted. "Well, that's a first."

Her mother's crestfallen expression caused Wynter to regret her harsh tone. "Listen, Mother, what do you want from me? I don't belong. For years, I have tried to fit my round peg in the square hole of this family and come out wanting. I'm tired of trying. I'm tired of trying to please you. It's not good for me. It has made me miserable for too many years, and I refuse to give you or anyone else that sort of power over me. It stops today."

"Wynter, I never knew you felt this way."

"C'mon, Mom. I've always done things your way, and you're always critical of everything I do. Growing up, I could never do anything right. All you ever did was praise Corey and his genius while I was the screwup."

"I'm sorry," her mother said. "I'm sorry I made you feel that way."

"It wasn't just you. It was Dad and Corey," Wynter responded. "I've never felt good enough. Or wanted, for that matter. I've felt invisible in this family."

"Why have you never spoken up before now?"

"I couldn't!" Wynter yelled. "Why do you think I

left? I left to escape the negativity and to find my own voice, without my family in my ear. I needed to find out who I was, and I did. But you don't know her. I don't think you ever did."

"I would like to know her now. Do you think it's possible to start over?" her mother asked. "Or try and find a middle ground? I know I'm not the perfect parent. Look how I've behaved about this will—once I started on this path, it just gained steam and took on a life of its own. I don't need the money, Wynter. I never have. I guess it just stung not being acknowledged by my sister, and I was angry and jealous and bitter. But I had no right to take it out on you. And I'm sorry."

Tears slid down Wynter's cheeks at her mother's confession. It was the most honest they'd ever been with each other. "I'm not the same Wynter that I was a few months ago. I've changed. I'm stronger, and I won't accept your indifference and Corey's animosity. I just wanted to be loved. It's all I have ever wanted."

"I do love you, Wynter. I may suck at showing it, but I do. Please forgive me." And to Wynter's utter surprise, her mother held open her arms and she rushed into them. It was a shock to the system, and at first, Wynter thought she was dreaming, but when her mother laid her head down on hers, she knew it wasn't a dream.

They were finally on the road to reconciliation.

# Fifteen

"Riley, I'm so glad you could come so quickly," Derek said when Riley arrived at the billionaire's home in an exclusive part of San Antonio later that day. As usual, the dark-haired man was dressed in jeans and graphic T-shirt and a pair of Nike Air Yeezy sneakers.

"Of course," Riley stated. "Your voice mail sounded urgent. What can I do to help? Has something happened with your ex-wife?"

"Yeah, it has," Derek said, lowering his voice. "If you don't mind, I'd like to talk to you in my study."

Riley followed him into a bright room decorated in muted blues and grays. The furniture was minimalistic and included a large desk and a laptop, along with a single lamp.

Derek glanced around him. "I'm renting this place

temporarily while we sort out the divorce. If I bought another place, it would be considered community property."

"No worries. Your interior design skills are not why I'm here. I take it your wife has made a move?"

"Damn right, she has," Derek said. "She's all but moved her trainer into the house where she lives with my son—while spending my money! Max tells me they are up all hours of the day and night, partying, drinking and Lord knows what else. They've already run off half the staff, so sometimes Max has to scrounge up dinner for himself. This is ridiculous! We need to go to court now to get temporary custody."

"I couldn't agree with you more." Riley hated hearing about a child with an incompetent parent. Parents were supposed to love and care for their children, not leave them to fend for themselves. He remembered what it was like when Eliza couldn't get out of bed and he'd had to cook and clean for himself and Shay. He didn't want that for Max or any child. "We'll file for an emergency hearing immediately."

Derek released a huge sigh. "Thank you, Riley. I appreciate it."

"Of course. That's what I'm here for."

After getting more information from Derek, Riley headed straight back to the office, where he stayed for the remainder of the afternoon until the paperwork was ready. Then his assistant rushed off before the court closed to file the documents. When it was over, Riley leaned back in his chair. This case brought up a lot of memories. Bad memories of growing up. He'd thought he'd handled them, but maybe Wynter was right. He needed to let it out, talk about it.

He hated emotions. They were messy. After the childhood he'd had, he liked tidy, with everything in its proper place. This case was certainly not ordered. Nearly half of his cases settled before they made it out of court, but he suspected this case was going to get ugly.

He was excited that he would be able to let it all go and find comfort in Wynter's arms tonight. They'd spent the entire week in Aspen and their first night back together and both agreed to a bit of a breather. Riley wasn't ashamed to admit that the space helped him gain control again.

Just one week with Wynter had been a game changer. He missed seeing her smile, hearing her laughter, smelling that sweet, heady scent that was uniquely hers. However, he knew if they hadn't taken some time apart, the feelings he'd started to feel in Aspen but usually kept at bay might have taken over, and that scared him most of all. He would have to reinforce the gates and pray Wynter didn't breach them with her warm and caring nature—because he wasn't ready to let her go.

"I'm so happy you and your mother had a good talk," Riley said when he stopped by Helaine's estate later that evening. He'd gotten tied up at work but had finally made it over there. And when he had, he'd given her a hot, passionate kiss that caused her toes to curl. She hadn't realized how much she'd missed him this past week.

"Yeah, it was," Wynter said. "It was so surprising. And not just about the inheritance. I think both of us allowed pride to get in the way and we both refused to budge. Instead, we let months go by and allowed the resentment to fester."

"What made you decide to give up half the money?" Riley asked. "You were entitled to the whole sum."

"Money doesn't mean everything to me," Wynter said. "It never has. My parents, my brother—they were always trying to fill their world up with things. I care about people. I want the Six Gems and all of my aunt's staff to get what they deserve. So what if I get a little bit less? I have this beautiful home—" she spread her arms out "—I'm not poor."

"That's what I admire about you, Wynter. How warm and giving you are," Riley said, pulling her into his lap and softly brushing his lips across hers. "I don't think I've ever met a woman like you."

"That's because I'm an original," Wynter said with a smile.

"That you are," Riley said, cradling her face in his hands.

Wynter was reminded once again why her life was so much sweeter with Riley in it. Maybe he was coming around yet; maybe forever wasn't out of the question.

The next few weeks floated by, and Wynter began to enjoy life in San Antonio again. She loved staying at Aunt Helaine's estate. Hope made her life so easy. She didn't have to cook or make her own bed. All she had to do was work on *Wynter's Corner*. With the blog's success, advertising offers were pouring in. If this continued, she would need to hire someone. She was giving a lot of thought to expanding her blog into a full online travel magazine. Though she did like to occasionally join Hope in the garden Hope started nearly three months ago, in her aunt's memory. Wynter loved the idea and often tried to help, though she did not have a green thumb.

That wasn't the only bright spot in Wynter's life; she and her mother met for coffee occasionally, and they were slowly starting to get reacquainted. Then, of course, there was Shay; she had a lot of ideas about the new studio she wanted to build. Would it be cycling only? Did she want yoga and Pilates? Wynter was glad she could be there to listen and dispense advice.

And then there was Riley. He was easy to be with and to say yes to. Desire between them continued to be strong. She'd thought maybe she was being fanciful about their relationship, but as weeks passed, they were still connected. Her body just wanted his. All the time. She wanted his kiss, his touch and everything in between.

In only one week, she would head off to meet the girls in Barbados. She'd come over to Riley's this time so Hope could have the night off. If she was in residence, Hope felt compelled to cook. Tonight, though, Wynter had tried her hand at cooking. She couldn't make much, but spaghetti and pasta sauce were pretty hard to mess up. She'd even asked Hope for a few pointers, and voilà, the meal wasn't a disaster.

The pasta was perfectly al dente, and the sauce tasted great thanks to the extra spices and fresh herbs she'd added. Riley ate every bit of it, all the while talking to her about how happy Derek was now that Riley had garnered him temporary custody of Max. Apparently, the first hearing had been pretty vicious, but the Shark of the East was victorious. Now, they were lounging on the sofa, eating chocolate ice cream.

"That was very good for a neophyte," Riley said, patting his belly.

She slapped his chest. "Don't sound so surprised."

"Hey," he said, laughing, "no fair. You were the one who told me you don't cook."

"I'm not great," Wynter said, "but I can scramble an egg."

"Good to know, but I'm not with you for your cooking," Riley said, taking both their bowls and placing them on the cocktail table nearby.

"Oh, no?" she inquired, raising a brow.

He shook his head and then rubbed his thumb against her bottom lip. Wynter sucked in a deep breath when he lifted it long enough for her to see a smear of chocolate on his finger. He licked it off, never taking his eyes off her.

"Riley…"

An arc of electricity went through her, and Riley instinctively knew what she needed, pulling her into his arms. She felt the fierce passion of his kiss as he plundered her with untamed desire. It didn't take long for them to retire to his bedroom, where their clothes melted away as Riley took her from the edge all the way to oblivion.

Sometime during the night or the next morning—Wynter didn't know which—Riley reached for her, and he was already protected. They didn't speak. There were just gasps and groans of pleasure and encouragement, and then he was settling between her thighs. His gaze held hers, and when their bodies merged, Wynter swore it felt as if she was coming home. They held each other's gaze for infinitesimal seconds, but then the need to move became overwhelming and Riley began to thrust rhythmically inside her.

When he held her hip and tilted her to meet him, Wynter arched her back as the pressure began to build to a powerful crescendo. She clung to his wide shoulders, taking him deeper, as if it were possible to take him to the very heart of her. Her brain scrambled and a maelstrom of emotions, from the glorious to the sublime, hit her. Riley must have felt the same, because his control shattered and they both cried out simultaneously. She gasped, shuddered and quaked as wave after wave, ripple after ripple, of pleasure engulfed her.

It was always this way with them. The bond, not just their physical connection, was so strong that Wynter knew without a shadow of a doubt that she'd fallen for this incredible, smart, funny, sexy man. And he seemed to be falling for her, too. He was everything she'd ever wanted. A high school crush had morphed into so much more because she'd gotten to know the real man underneath the facade.

With their hearts beating in unison, Wynter finally felt like she could say it, could reveal her true feelings. Their mouths were fused together and their bodies were still clinging to one another. Their bodies, minds and souls were in sync, so she said the words aloud. "I love you, Riley."

Riley tensed above her, as if Wynter had tossed a bucket of cold water on him, and then, to her surprise, he tossed off the covers and moved away from her.

Wynter knew then she had made a grave mistake. She was about to lose the man she loved.

* * *

Riley should have known this was going to happen given how intimate they'd been the past month. Was it any wonder Wynter thought it equated to love? But Riley was incapable of loving another human being who wasn't a member of his family. He wouldn't allow it. He'd always made sure his casual sex partners understood they couldn't expect anything in return, because he wasn't willing to risk his heart.

"Look… Wynter." He lowered his eyes. "You're confusing passion with feelings."

"Don't tell me how I feel!" Wynter replied.

"Then what do you expect me to say? That I love you, too? I've been honest with you from the beginning about what I can give." He heard her sharp intake of breath at his words and glanced up to see her eyes fill with tears.

"I want more," she said and slid from the bed with a sheet wrapped around herself as she began looking around the room for her clothes.

"You don't have to leave, Wynter. It's the middle of the night. Stay, we can talk."

"Why? I already feel like a fool," Wynter replied, picking up her dress and shoes. "I don't need you to bury the knife in my heart any further."

"I'm sorry, Wynter. I thought you understood this for what it was, a casual relationship—an incredible one," Riley responded with a wry smile. "I told you early on—"

Wynter held up her hand. "Please spare me. I remember, okay, but I thought that was before we…" She stopped speaking, and he could only assume she meant *fell in love.*

She brushed past him toward the bathroom, and he stopped her. "Wynter, please. Try to understand. I can't do the love and marriage thing. I've seen the devastating effects it can have, and I refuse to put myself through that."

"That's because you're scared, Riley. Why are you afraid of putting yourself out there and loving another person? Surely, after the last few weeks we've spent together in and out of bed, you feel something for me?"

"Of course, I do. I care for you a great deal, Wynter. Haven't I been there for you with everything that went down with your family? This isn't easy for me, either. I don't want to hurt you."

"Then why are you doing this? I know that loving someone comes with great risk because you're not sure if the other person reciprocates, but even so, at least I'm willing to try. Why aren't you willing to give us a chance?"

"Because I don't believe in happily ever after, Wynter. I can't give you what you're looking for—what you need."

Wynter shook her head because she couldn't understand the words coming out of his mouth. "You may not have told me you loved me, but your actions made me think otherwise. I can see I was a fool."

Wynter wrenched her arm free of his grasp and rushed to the en suite. Riley went to the closed door and placed his hand over it. He sensed Wynter on the other side. Sensed her agony and heard her crying, but he couldn't open the door to go to her. She was looking for a man who could give her a happily-ever-after, and he wasn't the man for her.

She deserved someone who wasn't damaged. Someone who could love her the way she deserved to be loved. And that man wasn't him. Or, at least, he didn't want it to be. Even though a part of him wished he were. She was right. He was dead inside. He'd walled himself off from any feeling or emotion after seeing his mother sob for his father night after night. After seeing her unable to shower and get dressed, let alone brush her teeth.

Love hurt, and Riley refused to be another victim.

He heard the shower run, and then, ten minutes later, Wynter emerged from the bathroom. Her cheeks were tearstained and her eyes red and puffy, but she didn't look at him. Instead, he watched as she found her purse.

He couldn't let her walk out. Not like this.

He followed her to the door, and when she went to open it, he closed it. "Wynter, if you leave here with nothing else, please know that I care for you."

When she finally glanced up at him, her light brown eyes were filled with hurt, and Riley hated that he was the cause of her pain. "Care for me? You couldn't. Because if you did, you wouldn't do this to me."

"I'm so sorry."

"You shouldn't be," Wynter said. "Because of you, I've realized I am special. I deserve to be recognized, loved and wanted by someone, and if that person isn't you, so be it. But I am going to tell you something."

"What's that?" Riley asked quietly.

"I'm the best thing that ever happened to you, Riley Davis, and you will regret letting me go."

Wynter swatted away his hand, walked out of the room and slammed the door, leaving Riley staring after her, feeling desolate. He had to wonder—*was she right?* Had he made the biggest mistake of his life?

# Sixteen

"Egypt," Wynter cried and flung herself in her best friend's arms later that evening. Even though she was due to meet her friends in Barbados in a week, after Riley's rejection, Wynter hadn't known where else to go. No one else but Egypt knew about their Aspen affair. She would understand and, sure enough, Egypt had welcomed her to her home in Raleigh, North Carolina.

"Come in," Egypt said, leading Wynter to the sofa in her one-bedroom apartment, which reflected Egypt's personality: bold colors, a zebra-print rug and comfy microsuede couch, a kitchen with pots and pans hanging down from the ceiling.

Egypt came beside Wynter and pulled her into her embrace. "Tell me what's happened. I couldn't make heads or tails of what you said at the airport."

"I'm sorry." Wynter sniffed into a Kleenex. She'd

been in full meltdown mode on the plane, so much so that one of the flight attendants had asked if she was okay. Wynter had informed her that she'd broken up with her boyfriend and was dealing with a broken heart. The attendant had understood and comped her a drink. Wynter had guzzled the beverage in one gulp. It had taken off the edge and calmed her enough to get through the rest of the flight until she could make it to Raleigh.

"It's okay. I'm just surprised, I thought you guys were happy together," Egypt inquired, tucking her legs underneath her.

Wynter shook his head. "Oh, he was happy with the sex, but love? No. He doesn't love me." And she wanted it all. It wasn't just about spectacular sex anymore. She'd been prepared to give him everything, all of herself, but he didn't want her.

"Just because he doesn't realize what a gem he has doesn't mean you're not worthy of love."

"I know that," Wynter responded even though Egypt wore a disbelieving expression. "I do. If being with Riley taught me anything, it showed me I'm worthy of love."

"Yes, you are."

"I will no longer tolerate being ignored or accepting less than I deserve, whether it's from Riley or my parents. For too long, I accepted the crumbs they offered, content to be in the background, to be invisible. Not anymore."

Egypt smiled broadly. "I'm glad to hear you say this, Wynter. You've allowed your family and other people to treat you less than kindly."

Her friend was right. After having been starved of

her parents' affection, attention and love, for once, she wanted to be the center of someone's universe. And for a short time, she'd felt that way with Riley. When they made love, it hadn't just been the sensual power of his body, though his body did rival that of any Greek god. Instead, it had been a physical expression of her love.

"Well, that stops now. I am stronger," Wynter replied. "But it still hurts, ya know? I thought, after all the time we spent together, in and out of bed, that he was developing feelings for me. That last day, the sex was so intense—the way he looked at me." Fresh tears sprang to her eyes, and Egypt reached for more Kleenex and handed it to her. Wynter took several tissues, blotted her eyes and blew her nose. "I—I misinterpreted it— thought I meant more to him."

"It happens," Egypt said. "We get so caught up in a man when we're falling in love and they're just having good sex. But that doesn't mean you were wrong to open your heart. One day, your true love will come."

"I never knew you were such a romantic, Egypt. I thought you were a realist."

"I'm both. I take what men say at face value and try not to read between the lines, but it doesn't mean I don't wish for a Prince Charming to sweep me off my feet."

"It will happen for you, my friend." Wynter reached across the sofa and squeezed her hand. "You are so deserving."

"And so are you," Egypt replied, patting her thigh. "What do you say we drown ourselves in some stiff drinks? I have some brandy in the kitchen I keep for recipes."

"I do need a libation." Wynter laughed and followed

Egypt into the kitchen, but in the back of her mind, she couldn't forget the look in Riley's eyes as she'd left. It was as if he'd been hurt, too, that she was leaving, when *he* was the reason she'd walked away. It didn't make any sense.

Wynter sighed. She had to stop thinking about Riley and how he might be feeling. He'd hurt her with his refusal to take a chance on love. They could have had a good thing, but now they would never know, because he'd been too afraid to take a risk.

"How's Wynter?" Derek asked Riley when he stopped by Derek's rental several days later to check on him now that he had custody of his son. It was important to Riley that the child had time to adjust after what he'd been through with his mother.

However, hearing Wynter's name caused Riley's heart to race. She was gone because he'd sent her away, because he'd not allowed emotion to overrule him. He refused to be like his mother. He'd seen the effect of her tumultuous emotions on him and Shay and how it had toppled her.

He thought about lying to Derek, but he and the billionaire had formed a good relationship, so he decided to be honest. "We broke up."

"Broke up?" Derek's shocked expression said it all. "Why? She's an amazing woman."

"I agree," Riley said, "but…" He couldn't bring himself to say the words.

"She's in love with you," Derek surmised. "You don't share her feelings?"

Riley nodded. He couldn't make her promises or

declarations of love. His father had done that, and he'd still walked out on their family and left him with his mentally unstable mother.

Derek regarded him and folded his arms across his chest. "Are you sure about that? Because the man I saw in Aspen was absolutely smitten with Ms. Barrington."

Riley shook his head. "You must be mistaken—I don't believe in love or marriage."

"So you say," Derek replied, peering at him intently. "But I suspect you're going to find out otherwise."

Later that evening, back at his penthouse, Riley wondered what Derek had meant. Although he missed Wynter's charm and wit and, of course, the passion they shared in bed, Riley told himself he'd made the right decision. He had freed her from the notion she could change him. Someday she would find a man who could love her and give her a ring. He wasn't that man. Romantic love wasn't part of his life. Period.

But he had wanted Wynter like he had never wanted anyone. She intrigued and excited him in equal measure. He missed her terribly, and that was the most surprising part. He couldn't stop thinking about her. Why had she asked for *more?* Why had she wanted him to express his feelings? For years, he'd cut himself off from feeling anything. When his casual relationships ended, it was on to the next case or the next woman to warm his bed. And yet, he couldn't deny he felt different now, changed somehow, and it was all because of Wynter.

"Wynter, you outdid yourself," Asia gushed when they arrived at the two-story home situated in Holetown, Saint James, on the coast of Barbados.

"Thanks," Wynter said as she gave the Gems a tour of their whitewashed vacation rental, which had direct beachfront access and included four bedrooms, four baths and a splash pool.

"It has all the amenities," Teagan said, whipping off the wide-brimmed hat she'd worn on the ride over in the large Escalade they'd rented for the week.

The top floor of the home had colonial-style furniture and a large, modern and well-equipped kitchen, and it boasted wood flooring throughout, including all the bedrooms. The downstairs had another bedroom, which overlooked the garden, as well as the living area, which offered a pool table, day beds and even a hammock.

"This is paradise." Lyric kicked off her shoes and plopped down on one of the sofas in the living room.

"How about we get this party started?" Egypt asked. "We need to do a store run and get all the essentials."

"Already done." Wynter went to the cabinets. She opened each one up to reveal an array of wines, spirits and mixers. Then she went to the fridge, which was fully stocked.

"Oh, my God! I love you," Egypt said, pulling Wynter into a one-armed hug. Once she released her, she reached for the blender on the countertop and took out the ingredients needed to make a margarita.

"You're welcome." Wynter smiled and moved away to walk outside onto the covered deck overlooking the ocean. The owners had thought of everything; comfy white sofas covered by pillows decorated with green leaves greeted her there.

The terrace had a stunning view of the garden, with its lush palm trees and colorful plants. Below her, Wynter saw six loungers for sunbathing and a pool set off to the side. A rejuvenating stay was exactly what she needed after the horrible week she'd endured. She'd been sleeping on Egypt's sofa and crying on her shoulder every night as she recalled every waking minute of her short-lived affair with Riley. She intended to tell the rest of her friends this week, but she wasn't looking forward to Shay's response in particular.

Wynter knew Shay wouldn't be happy with her for not heeding her advice, but it was Riley. The man she'd crushed on since she was a teen. Meeting him as an adult changed *everything*, and she'd allowed herself to fall harder and deeper than she had with other men.

As if sensing her distress, Shay came toward her. "What's on your mind, Wynter?" she inquired. "You don't seem yourself."

"How can I not be, in a place like this?" Wynter asked, motioning with her arms.

"You don't fool me, Wynter Barrington." Shay leaned her back against the balustrade. "You've never been good at disguising your emotions. Something is bothering you. You can talk to me—to any of us." She inclined her head toward the kitchen, where the rest of the women were gathered around Egypt as she made their adult beverages.

Wynter offered Shay a small smile. "There is, but if it's all the same, I'm not ready to talk about it."

Shay nodded. "All right, but I'm here if you need me."

Wynter nodded. "Thank you." She was thankful when Shay quietly moved away and left her alone with her thoughts. She knew she would have to pull herself out of her slump and carry on. She was struggling to write, because, every time she did, memories of her and Riley filled her mind.

*Was he feeling the pain as acutely as she was?*

Wynter doubted it. He probably didn't feel anything at all.

Riley had had a devil of a time over the past week. He'd arrived late to an appointment and stumbled in court on a case that should have been a walk in the park. Opposing counsel came at him hard, and Riley had barely been able to string two sentences together. He felt discombobulated.

The nights were worse. He was restless and couldn't sleep. Every night, he stared at the ceiling and prayed for sleep, but it wouldn't come. Why? Because every time he closed his eyes, he saw Wynter. Wynter on the snowmobile. Wynter laughing on the thrilling dogsled ride. Wynter licking ganache off a spoon. Wynter in the mirror when he fingered her and made her come as she rode his stiff length.

This was ridiculous!

He had always been able to compartmentalize his feelings with other women and keep them in check. He had never been in emotional danger with any of them, because it had never been more than a physical connection. But now, looking out over the San Antonio skyline from his penthouse, his jaw shadowed with today's growth, Riley felt different.

Because *he* was different. Somehow Wynter, with her beautiful brown eyes, warm smile and giving nature, had breached the walls he'd erected around his heart and found her way in. She made him come alive in a way he'd never imagined. Joy and light had burst into his life the moment he'd seen her sitting on the River Walk, and it hadn't left. In their short time together, something invisible yet strong had melded to his central framework and become inseparable from his soul. It was Wynter. She was lodged here. Riley put his hand on his heart. She was a part of him.

The thought of what that something invisible was, that rare element that threaded them together, scared Riley. He was afraid to name it, didn't want to say it aloud, but he knew. Deep down, he knew.

It was love.

Despite him fighting it and pushing Wynter away, somehow love had found its way in and now resided in his heart. Riley rubbed his hand over his closely cropped hair.

What was he supposed to do now? He'd ruined any chance he had with Wynter when he shot her down after she'd professed her love for him. He'd said hurtful things to her in an effort to push her away and negate the emotions he'd seen shining back at him through her tearful eyes. Riley wasn't sure if he could live with this feeling and not say anything. He had to tell her, but would she ever listen to him? And why would she? She owed him nothing. He'd made sure of that.

But maybe, just maybe, deep down in the recesses of her heart, was there a place that still loved him? Riley had to find out. He wouldn't quit until she forgave him, because he always won. But this was different. He wasn't helping someone give up on love. This time, he would be fighting for it.

# Seventeen

With blue skies overhead, fresh air and her friends by her side, Wynter felt good. Losing Riley had nearly flattened her, but then her mother dropped the challenge to the will officially with the courts and the article she'd written for the Aspen resort was a success. So much so, the luxury chain had asked her to write other pieces for them. This would do great things for *Wynter's Corner* and would allow Wynter the freedom and independence she craved.

Wynter spent the remaining time enjoying her friends' company. They swam in the pool, sunbathed on the loungers, went horseback riding on the beach and ate delicious food from the private chef she'd arranged to stop by several times during their stay. Their favorite meal had consisted of authentic Bahamian dishes, including cou-cou and flying fish, pepperpot and brown stew chicken with rice and peas. Egypt couldn't stop raving about the food and vowed to attempt to cook it herself when they returned to the States.

Now they found themselves at the Barbados straw market on Broad Street, where Egypt walked up and down the aisles picking up spices from this vendor and the next. Wynter was content to peruse the usual tourist fare of T-shirts, shot glasses, magnets and the like. She was holding up T-shirts and deciding which one to pick when Shay came up beside her.

"I like that one," Shay said, motioning to a black T-shirt printed with the blue-and-yellow Barbados flag.

Wynter nodded. She was leaning toward that one, too. "So do I. You know me so well." She pulled out her wallet and handed the vendor ten dollars.

Afterward, she and Shay continued walking down the aisle. Shay linked her arm with one of Wynter's. "And because I know you, I can say that you appear to be doing better than when we first arrived."

Wynter gave Shay a sideward glance. "I am."

"Are you finally ready to confide in me?"

Wynter sighed. She was. But Wynter was going to need some liquid courage, because she was certain Shay would be upset by the news. Asia, Lyric and Teagan wouldn't be happy, either, that she hadn't told them.

"Soon." Wynter patted Shay's arm that was linked with hers.

Later that evening, Egypt found Wynter in the kitchen. "What was up with you and Shay earlier?"

Wynter glanced around to see if they were alone. "She wanted to know why I've been in such a funk."

"Did you tell her about Riley?" Egypt inquired.

The moment Egypt said his name, Shay walked into the kitchen. "What about Riley?" Shay looked from one woman to the other.

Egypt hung her head low. "Oh, Lord, the shit is about to hit the fan."

"Shay…" Wynter started toward Shay, but her friend was backing up.

"Riley? You and Riley have been seeing each other?" Shay inquired. "For how long? Since the funeral?"

Wynter followed her and stood in the middle of the living room, ready to tell her truth to the remaining Six Gems. "No. Well…" She realized they had had the one-night stand. If she was going to be honest, she had to tell them everything.

"Well, what?" Shay asked.

"After the funeral, we had a one-night stand," Wynter replied, wringing her hands.

"Oh, my!" Asia clutched the junky necklace she'd purchased at the straw market as if she were clutching her pearls.

Wynter glared at Asia. "We both said it was going to be the one night, but then…" She lowered her head, and when she glanced up at Egypt, she gave her a nod to continue.

Shay caught the action and looked at Egypt with a sharp stare. "Did you know about this?"

Egypt shrugged. "I did. But if it wasn't going to amount to anything, I saw no reason for Wynter to tell you about it."

"She should have told me because we're friends!" Shay countered. Then she turned to Wynter. "Go on."

"When I arrived in Aspen, Riley was there, and the

chemistry between us was still there. We spent the week together, and then afterwards, when we came back to San Antonio, we continued seeing each other. And I—I fell in love with your brother, but he didn't feel the same way. He told me he would never love me and wasn't capable or willing to try."

Shay sighed. "Oh, Wynter." To Wynter's surprise, she came forward and gave her a hug. "I'm so sorry. I warned you about him." She released her long enough to grasp both of Wynter's cheeks with her palms. "Riley was traumatized by our parents' divorce and swore off love and marriage."

Tears slid down Wynter's cheeks. "I know... I guess I thought, after our time together..."

"He would change?" Shay offered. "I hope he does one day, because you deserve love, Wynter. You always have."

Wynter offered a half smile. "Thank you. And I'm sorry I didn't tell you about us."

"It's okay," Shay said and wiped one of her tears with her thumb. "No man, my brother included, will tear us Gems apart. We vowed years ago that our sisterhood was unbreakable. That hasn't changed."

*"Aw!"* Asia cried, and before Wynter knew it, all the ladies were in a group hug, holding each other tight.

After they released one another, Egypt said, "Now all this lovey-dovey stuff is over, don't you think it's time we celebrate? Your mom dropped the case! We're getting our inheritance from Auntie Helaine!"

"Woo-hoo!" Asia began popping her bottom up and down in a little dance.

It was Teagan who went to the kitchen. When she

returned, she was holding a bottle of champagne and six plastic champagne flutes. Teagan handed each of the women a flute and popped the cork, pouring each of them a glass. Once they were filled, she said, "Here's to Auntie Helaine and opening our own businesses."

"To Aunt Helaine." They toasted and drank the delicious champagne.

The celebration continued well into the night, when they all retired to the terrace to listen to the waves and discuss their upcoming ventures. In the months they'd been waiting for the will to be resolved, Teagan had obtained her brokerage license and was prepared to start her new real estate firm. Egypt, having already secured a location for her new restaurant, was retiring her food truck. Based on the private dance lessons she was currently giving, Lyric had compiled a list of students for her new dance studio. Shay's built-in clientele from the yoga and Pilates classes vowed to follow her to her own studio. Meanwhile, Asia's jewelry had been selling out at farmers markets and online, and she couldn't wait to have her own store.

"This is great and exactly what my aunt wanted for each of you," Wynter responded after hearing their updates. "I'm so proud of all of you." And thankful to her aunt for giving them the opportunity to follow their dreams.

"What about you, Wynter?" Lyric asked. "What's next for you?"

That was the million-dollar question. Wynter had done a lot of soul-searching during her travels, so she knew what she wanted to do next. "I'm going to start my own online travel magazine."

"That sounds fantastic!" Teagan said brightly. "But what about *Wynter's Corner*?"

"I'm not giving it up entirely, because I'll still give my insights on various destinations, but I plan on incorporating them into the magazine," Wynter replied. "And I'll hire a staff to help me write the articles. For now, I'd like to sit in one place and smell the roses. I have a home now." Her aunt's home was now officially hers. "I want to plant some roots."

Egypt nodded and gave her a wide smile. "Sounds like a mighty fine idea to me."

"Thank you, love." Wynter thought so, too. And when she got back to San Antonio, things were going to change. First, she would continue to try to heal the rift between her and her parents; she'd already made progress with her mother.

As for Riley, she would always treasure the moments they'd shared—the way he'd laughed with her, kissed her, made love to her—but she would have to store them in a vacuum-sealed part of heart until time passed and it no longer hurt so much.

She should thank him, though. He'd freed her from the shroud of being hidden and staying safe in the shadows. Spending time with him had made her want more. Want love. He might not love her, and she couldn't force him to. Instead of pining for something that couldn't be, she was moving on with her life.

One day, she would find love again. She just didn't know when.

# Eighteen

Riley pulled into the parking lot of a strip mall in a popular part of town to meet Shay. From what he heard, all the yuppies and new families were flocking here, but he had no idea why Shay would be here. Did she have news to tell him?

Turning off the ignition, he exited the vehicle and headed to the suite number Shay had given him. When he tried the door, it opened freely to a wide-open retail space with a bare concrete floor.

"Shay?"

His sister emerged several moments later from the rear of the suite. "What do you think?" Her eyes were gleaming with excitement.

"About what?"

"About this place for my yoga and Pilates studio?" Shay asked as if he were a mind reader.

"So, Wynter's family officially dropped the case with the courts and the estate will be dispersing funds?" Just saying her name again made his newly recognized feelings rise to the surface. Feelings he hadn't been able to share because Wynter had been in Barbados with his sister.

Plus, he hadn't figured out the best approach to win her back.

"That's right," Shay replied with a wide smile.

"Really? That's fantastic!" Riley reached for Shay and swung her around. He was happy for Wynter. She would finally get her inheritance and her aunt's employees and charities would finally get the bequests they were entitled to.

When he released her, Shay looked at him. "You sound awfully happy for Wynter."

Riley gave a small smile. "Well, um, I saw how devastated she was after the funeral and…"

"Stop!" Shay held up her hand.

His brows knitted into a frown. "Stop what?"

"Stop with the lies," Shay said, poking her finger at his chest. "I know the truth, Riley. I know about you and Wynter in Aspen." And when Riley tried to interrupt her, she added, "And I know about the one-night stand, too. And your time together in San Antonio."

Riley lowered his head. He supposed he shouldn't be surprised. Wynter and Shay were best friends. How long would she have been able to keep something like that from her best friend, especially when she was hurting? And Riley knew she was. He'd seen the devastation in her eyes when she'd left his penthouse.

"Shay, I'm sorry."

"For which part? For sleeping with Wynter or for breaking her heart?" Shay glared at him. He hated seeing the disappointment in her eyes.

"For breaking her heart, of course," Riley responded. "I never wanted to hurt Wynter, but I did anyway. I regret that."

"That's good to hear. I would hate to think my brother is one of those men who only want one thing."

"Our relationship was more than just sex, Shay. We joked and teased each other. We could talk about anything. We had fun together in the snow in Aspen. We had more fun together here."

Shay shook her head. "Then why—why did you let her go?" she asked, her pitch rising several octaves.

"Because I'm a fool," Riley yelled back. "I didn't realize what I had until she was gone."

Shay's expression softened, and she walked toward him and touched his arm. "I suspected you'd met someone, because your entire demeanor was different when we spoke while you were in Aspen, and then later back home."

"You could tell?"

She nodded.

"I was afraid, then, of the feelings Wynter was evoking inside me. I don't want to end up like our mother, Shay. She was devastated by losing Dad. We lost her for so long."

"I know, Riley," Shay said, cupping his cheek, "but you're not Mom. Marriage is what *you* make it. Don't you see? Love is not a weakness, it's your greatest strength, but you have to allow it to happen."

"How can you still believe in love after your divorce?"

Shay shrugged. "Kevin may not have been my person, but that doesn't mean the institution of marriage is flawed. It means I made a mistake, but I'm not giving up on love."

"What do I do now, Shay? I want her back."

Shay chuckled. "Of course you do. Wynter is an amazing woman, but you've got an uphill battle. She's angry and hurt. I'm not sure how you're going to repair the damage you caused."

"I don't know, either, but I have to try. Will you help me?"

Shay looked upward and rubbed her chin.

"Hmm…let me think about it."

"Shay, please."

"Of course I'll help you," Shay replied. "Listen, Wynter is going to her parents' anniversary party on Saturday. You should go."

She wouldn't be expecting him, which gave Riley the advantage. He just prayed it wasn't too late to win his woman back.

As soon as she'd landed in San Antonio and returned to her aunt's after Barbados, Wynter had found an embossed invitation to attend her parents' thirtieth wedding anniversary celebration that week. Although her relationship with her mother had thawed, Wynter hadn't been up to forging a path of forgiveness with her father, brother and Francesca in the weeks before Barbados, but she knew she had to if she wanted peace in the family. She'd checked yes on the reply card.

The day of the event, however, she thought about chickening out, but it was Egypt who gave her a good pep talk over the phone.

"Do you recall telling the Gems you were going to demand what you're worth and no longer accept what your parents, Riley or anyone else dished out?"

"I didn't realize I was on the witness stand," Wynter replied.

Egypt laughed. "You're not, but I want you to remember the new, improved Wynter you've become. If I could, I'd go with you."

"It's okay," Wynter said. "You're in the middle of construction on your restaurant. You can't afford to take your eye off the ball. I'm fine. I don't need a babysitter or a bodyguard. I'm going to put on my big-girl pant ies and handle my business."

"All right—are you sure?" Egypt asked. "I could call Shay for reinforcements."

"I told you. I've got this."

When evening arrived and the limo drove her toward her parents' house, Wynter's resolve to not let anyone get into her head tonight was starting to vanish. She reminded herself she wasn't a child in need of their love and acceptance anymore. She was a grown woman who was independently wealthy and didn't need anything from them.

Wynter was no longer dependent on her family for handouts. Even if she never received the money from her aunt's estate, Wynter had learned she could make a living and support herself with her blog. That had been the biggest revelation throughout the past few harrowing months. She'd found a strength she hadn't known she had.

Digging deep, Wynter called upon that reserve so when the limo pulled up outside her familial home, she was calm, cool and collected. Tonight, she wore a strapless red silk chiffon gown with a sweetheart neckline and a slim, draped skirt, accompanied by red peep-toe shoes and a sparkling gold clutch. She'd finished the look with a dazzling pair of gold earrings, kohl-rimmed eyes and a nude, shimmering lip. Wynter knew she looked her best and no one could find fault, though she wouldn't be surprised if someone in her family did.

Agnes wasn't there to greet the guests. Instead, there was a uniformed butler. Once inside, Wynter stood inside the foyer. The mansion looked familiar because she'd lived here for years, but it didn't feel like home anymore. She'd come to think of her aunt's place as *her* home, because it was where she had *always* belonged.

Wynter walked into the living room, and her parents immediately approached her. Her father looked debonair in a black tuxedo, while she could tell her mother had gone to great effort, because her hair was in a sophisticated updo and she wore a one-shouldered black dress with an enormous bow and a long train.

"Wynter!" Her mother's arms were outstretched, and she grasped both of her hands while her father lagged behind. "I'm so happy you came. It means a lot."

"Yes, it does," her father said, smiling at her. "A lot has happened."

"I agree, but I wouldn't miss your special day. Happy anniversary," Wynter replied, feigning a smile. "Thank you for inviting me."

"It would be bad etiquette if they didn't." Corey and Francesca joined their small circle. Her brother gave her a sardonic smile.

Wynter didn't bother to feign happiness at seeing him. "I see you haven't changed."

"But you have," Francesca replied. "You look amazing in that dress, Wynter, and your skin looks radiant, but, then again, you do have money at your disposal now."

"Thank you, Francesca. If you'll excuse me." Wynter didn't waste further time on her brother and his uppity wife. The time for her being the family's whipping post was over. She moved farther into the room to mingle.

She went to the bar and ordered a bourbon. She would need one to make it through this evening. The only reason she was here was to speak with her family. Once that was done, she was headed home to watch Netflix.

She was sipping her bourbon when her neck prickled. Only one person gave her that feeling—the feeling that she couldn't breathe. Wynter's eyes scanned the great room and connected with a pair of dark eyes. She tensed, and her heart beat painfully fast.

Riley.

He was wearing an all-black tuxedo and shirt and looked like a dark knight, but he was no longer her knight in shining armor. Why was he here, at her familial home? What did he want? Another romp in bed? And why now? It had been weeks and she was finally starting to be able to sleep without wishing his arms were wrapped around her.

She couldn't deal with this right now. She had mustered just enough energy to get through meeting with her family and nothing more. She threw back the rest of her drink and felt the burn in the back of her throat. Then she rushed out of the great room. She was down the hall when she heard loud voices from a nearby room. She recognized them.

It was her parents and her brother.

"Why can't you be nice to your sister?" her mother asked. "Is that too much to ask?"

"Why?" Corey asked. "You've never cared before. In fact, I think you both have always liked pitting both of us against each other. But now that Wynter has agreed to share Auntie's inheritance, you're going to kiss her ass? Is that why you invited her?"

Wynter flung open the door of the room. "I'd like to know the answer to that question." Startled, they all turned around to look at her. Her mother's expression was one of guilt. Was Corey right? Were they using her?

Wynter felt sick to her stomach and slowly began to step backward.

"Wynter, wait!"

"Why, Mother? So I can hear more lies?" Wynter asked. "Corey's right, isn't he? You brought me here so we could play happy family, but you don't really mean it, do you?"

"Of course we do," her father responded. "We wanted you to come tonight to heal this family and mend the rift between us."

"I never should have contested the will," her mother said. "I should have honored my sister's wishes, but I was so upset and angry with Helaine for choosing you instead of me that I took it out on you. It wasn't fair."

"No, it wasn't," Wynter responded. "But you've never treated me fairly." Wynter looked at her father. "And you've always looked down on me and treated me as if I wasn't good enough. As if I didn't belong."

"I know. I've been a terrible father, Wynter," he admitted. "Can you ever forgive me? I didn't know how to love you because my father was cold and distant, too, so I pushed you away, but I want to try now."

"I don't know," Wynter responded.

"It may be too soon, sweetheart, and we get that," her mother said. "We just hope, in time, you'll give us a chance to make things right. To be the parents you deserve."

Wynter stared at her parents and then at her brother, who was leaning against the wall as if he'd been hit by a Mack truck.

"And the money?" she asked.

"If you think I love money over you, you're wrong. You can take it all. The money is yours," her mother responded hotly. "Your aunt wanted you to have it, but it's not like you need it. I told your father how *Wynter's Corner* is a big hit."

"I'm proud of you, baby girl," her father said. "You did it all on your own, without any help. I wanted you to stand on your own two feet, and you did. Not that you should have had to, but you showed me and any other naysayers that you're a strong, independent woman."

That brought a smile to Wynter's face, but all wasn't forgiven yet. It would be a long time before she could say they were a happy family, but she supposed tonight was a start.

"So, now we've all kissed and made up," Corey said, "what's next? Singing 'Kumbaya'?"

Wynter spun around to face her brother. "Why do you hate me so much?"

"I don't hate you, Wynter," Corey said. "I never have. I'm jealous of you, and I supposed that's why I've always been so angry with you because you have been free to live your life without our parents'—" he flung his arms at their parents, who were watching the encounter in stunned silence "—expectations. You weren't the firstborn with all their hopes and dreams weighing down your shoulders. You've been free to figure out your own life, make mistakes and learn from them, while I've always had to walk the straight line."

"No offense, Mom and Dad—" she glanced in her parents' direction "—but who cares what they want? It's your life, Corey, and you have to live it on your own terms. And the first thing you can do is stop being an ass to your sister."

He stuck his chest out. "Is that right?"

"It is indeed. I'm stepping off my soapbox." She walked over to her parents and, to their surprise, gave them each a brief hug. "Happy anniversary." And then she swept out of the room.

She was so involved in her feelings that she didn't look in front of her and collided with a hard chest. Glancing up, she found Riley looking down at her.

"Wynter, can we talk?"

She shook her head. "I can't!" First her parents, then Corey, and now Riley—it was all too much for her to deal with in one night. "I just can't!"

"When, then?" Riley asked. "You pick the time and day."

This was new; Riley wasn't trying to control the situation. He was letting her take the lead. "All right, I'll call you."

She'd accepted his offer to talk for no other reason than for her own curiosity. She thought they'd said everything they had to say before she left for Barbados. What had changed? She still felt the same way. She still wanted love and commitment. Was that why he'd come? Was he no longer afraid? Was he finally ready to love?

# Nineteen

Riley felt terrible. He felt so bad he did something he'd never done in his entire career—he called out sick from work. How had he thought showing up to the Barrington estate on Saturday night was a good idea? It wasn't. He'd ambushed Wynter after telling her he didn't love her and never would.

*Was it any surprise that she ran away from him?*

He'd thought about chasing after her and pleading with her to listen, but he didn't. She needed her space. From the look on her face as she'd left that room, something had gone down between her and her parents. Something she hadn't been able to handle or verbalize. Damn them.

He'd assumed her family wanted to heal their relationship. If that was their version of healing, he would hate to see what happened when they ripped each other to shreds.

Yesterday, he'd stayed in bed and stared at the ceiling, wondering what he should do. How could he make things right? He was the fixer, after all. People paid him hundreds of thousands of dollars to fix their lives after their marriages fell apart. But now, when it was time for him to fix his own life, Riley felt ill-equipped to do so. Wynter had been right when she'd said he'd regret letting her go. He regretted being a coward and not opening himself fully to receive her love, which was a precious gift.

And now he was sitting outside a café alone on the River Walk, where he'd run into Wynter all those months ago. For what? In the hopes he might see her? And say what? *I'm sorry for being a jerk and turning my back on the best thing that ever happened to me.* Check. *Sorry for hurting you.* Check.

He was stunned when, several minutes later, Wynter did indeed come to the café, but rather than walk inside and place an order, she headed to his table. She looked sexy as hell in a maxi dress. It showed her cleavage, and Riley swallowed hard.

"Would you care for a walk?" she asked.

Riley's heart hammered loudly in his chest when her brown eyes pierced his. "I would love one." He tossed several bills on the table and joined her on the sidewalk.

They walked side by side for several minutes before Wynter stopped and turned to face him. "I'm sorry for running away the other night."

"You have nothing to apologize for," Riley responded. "*I* ambushed you."

She shook her head. "It's not that. It's just that I promised myself I was done running and I would face my problems head-on, but when put to the test, I ran. So, here I am. What did you want to talk to me about?"

Riley was proud of Wynter. She'd grown in the past several months and wasn't afraid to deal with her problems. He had to do the same thing. Inhaling deeply, he thought about the speech he had prepared on Saturday. An opening statement, if you will, but when he glanced down and saw Wynter's wary expression, he knew he had to speak straight from the heart. "Wynter, I'm sorry for the things I said to you at the penthouse."

"You don't have to apologize for being honest, Riley. It was my fault for thinking I could change you."

"Your love changed me."

At that bold statement, Wynter glanced up questioningly, so he continued, "For so long, I've been angry with my father for walking out on our family and my mother for falling apart after the divorce. Watching her pain, day after day, hurt. So, I began to see love as a sickness that needed to be cured. I never wanted the emotion and adamantly refused to have anything to do with love, but then I saw you sitting here on the River Walk and my heart expanded in a way it never had."

"I appreciated your kindness to me that night."

"It wasn't just kindness. I wanted you then as I want you now."

She shook her head. "Riley..."

"Please let me finish, Wynter." His heart was tight in his chest, as if iron bands were squeezing it. He had to tell her his feelings or he would burst. "I opened up to you and shared things about myself about being a workaholic and my history of choosing short-term relationships."

"Yes, you did, because you wanted me to know that I could never be more than just a fling. Well, guess what? These casual flings will never fill the hole deep inside you, Riley."

"No, they can't, because you have."

"Pardon?"

Riley reached for Wynter's hand, but she stepped away. He didn't blame her. He would have to earn her love. "I've been imprisoned by my past and carefully guarding my heart because I was afraid to fall in love, but my wise sister told me that love isn't a weakness, it's a strength. It made me realize I can't be a coward anymore, afraid of getting hurt because, like you said, I could be letting go of the best thing that ever happened to me. And no one ever said I'm not a smart man."

"What are you saying, Riley?"

"I'm saying that I love you." He waited for her reaction to the words because he rarely said them, but she was staring back at him with disbelief, so he repeated them again. "I love you, Wynter."

Wynter shook her head and clenched her hands into tight fists at her side. "Why are you saying these things? You told me you didn't believe in love."

"Because it's true, sweetheart," Riley replied softly. "I'm half a man without you. I can't sleep. I can't think. I can't work without you by my side. I won Derek's business because of *you*. Because you told me to speak from the heart about why I was the best attorney for him."

"I'm glad you won Derek over, but you don't have to say you love me when you don't mean it."

"Why don't you believe me?" Riley asked. "Because you don't think you're worthy? Because your parents haven't given you the love and affection you deserve? Well, I'm here to tell you, Wynter Barrington, you deserve all the love and happiness your heart and hands can hold."

Tears slipped down her cheeks, and that was when Riley knew she was finally hearing his words. He was starting to get through to her.

Wynter wanted to believe Riley and that all her dreams were coming true, but so many times she'd given her love to her family, and then to Riley, only to have tossed it aside. She was afraid to put her heart on the line again.

Riley grabbed both of Wynter's hands and brought her to an empty bench nearby. "You know as well as I do that we found something special on that first walk. You knew you could trust me. It's why, even though we hadn't seen each other in years, you asked me to sit with you at your aunt's funeral—because, intuitively, you knew could lean on me."

He was right about that. Her friends had thought she was crazy with grief when she asked Riley to sit beside her, but his presence had been a comfort when she needed it most.

"And later, when we made love, I didn't know it yet, but you ruined me. Ruined the old me," Riley said, "because I couldn't stop thinking about you. When we were apart, I was never with anyone else, because *you* were all I wanted."

"I was?"

"And when we came back together, I was made whole again," Riley replied. "Only to mess things up because I ran scared. You were right. I was a coward because I was afraid to feel. I told you I didn't believe in love, but it wasn't true. I do love you, Wynter. Please tell me it's not too late and I can have a do-over to make things right between us?"

Wynter nodded, her eyes filling with tears.

"I need to hear you say it, sweetheart."

"It's not too late, Riley," Wynter responded softly. "I've been enthralled with you since I was a teenager, and when I saw you after all these years, I was attracted to you and my feelings grew after our one night together, then grew again in Aspen and during our time together here. I tried pushing them aside, but, like you, I couldn't be intimate with anyone else because you already had my heart."

"Oh, thank God!" Riley leaned his forehead against hers, and Wynter stroked his cheek.

"I love you, Riley Davis."

Riley reached for her, pulling her close and kissing her with the fiery intensity he always did. Wynter answered the thrust of his tongue by mating it with hers in a playful duel that reminded Wynter she would never tire of kissing him.

When they finally parted, Riley lifted his head long enough to ask, "Will you marry me, Wynter?"

Wynter didn't hesitate, because her heart overflowed with love for this man. "Yes!" She threw her arms around Riley's neck and pulled him closer. They kissed until they shared the same air—shared the same breath. Because, in that moment, they were of the same heartbeat.

And later, when they were alone and Riley moved

over Wynter, joining them as one, it wasn't just their bodies fused together—it was their souls, in a love that would last a lifetime.

# Epilogue

*Six months later*

"Congratulations, Egypt!" Wynter said when she and Riley arrived at the opening of her best friend's restaurant, Flame, in Raleigh. They'd just flown in from San Antonio because court had ended late for Riley due to the final hearing for Derek's case. The Shark of the East had won. He'd not only been able to show how unfit Derek's ex-wife was, but they'd also found she'd been having an affair with her trainer for months. The prenup had expressly stated that she would forgo her settlement if infidelity occurred. Derek had not only been able to retain his company but had garnered full custody of his son, Max.

Riley was over the moon and had wanted to stay and celebrate with Derek, but knowing how important this night was and how much Wynter needed to be there, he'd chartered a private jet to ensure they made it on time.

Wynter handed her friend a large bouquet of flowers. "I'm so proud of you."

"Thank you so much." Egypt beamed with pride while accepting the arrangement. She looked like a professional restaurateur in her black chef's coat and simple updo.

"This is for you, too," Riley said, holding up an expensive bottle of bubbly. "Where should I put it?"

"Over there with the other gifts," Egypt said, indicating a small table with cards and wrapped gifts.

While he went to handle the gifts, Wynter grabbed Egypt's arm and linked it with hers. "Well, how do you feel?"

"Amazing. Scared. Overwhelmed," Egypt said. "What if I fail? Half of new restaurants fail in their first year."

*"Shh."* Wynter shook her head. "We are not going to claim that. Flame is going to be a success, and I'm not going to hear another negative word."

"That's right!" Shay said from behind them. She'd hitched a ride with them on the jet.

All the Six Gems were on hand to support Egypt as they always did. Egypt had been saving for the restaurant for a couple of years, but it would have taken much longer to open it without Aunt Helaine's endowment. Meanwhile, the rest of the Six Gems were still working through the particulars of starting their own businesses.

"I say we toast to Egypt," Teagan said, taking charge like she always did.

"Hear, hear!" the ladies cheered.

Soon, champagne and well-wishes were flowing. Wynter was thrilled to see everyone so happy.

She didn't even mind when Riley swept her into a secluded, dark corner and planted a searing kiss on her lips, because in a few short months, she was walking down the aisle to this incredible man and her happily-ever-after.

The past few months, their relationship had grown by leaps and bounds, because Riley had opened himself to feeling his emotions. Nowadays, it wasn't uncommon for him to express how much he loved her, because he knew that she would always be there. He might be her best friend's brother, but he'd stolen her heart years ago, and she'd never come close to loving another man the way she loved him.

"You're incredible," he whispered, and when he looked at her, she could see the love shining from his eyes.

She felt the same. Before him, she hadn't known where she fit in, but she did now. She belonged with Riley. He was her universe, and together, their love would have no bounds.

\* \* \* \* \*

*Look for the next Six Gems novel*
*Egypt's story*
*Coming summer 2023!*
*Only from Yahrah St. John and Harlequin Desire*

## #2923 ONE NIGHT RANCHER

*The Carsons of Lone Rock* • by Maisey Yates

To buy the property, bar owner Cara Thompson must spend one night at a ghostly hotel and asks her best friend, Jace Carson, to join her. But when forbidden kisses melt into passion, *both* are haunted by their explosive encounter...

## #2924 A COWBOY KIND OF THING

*Texas Cattleman's Club: The Wedding* • by Reese Ryan

Tripp Nobel is convinced Royal, Texas, is perfect for his famous cousin's wedding. But convincing Dionna Reed, the bride's Hollywood best friend...? The wealthy rancher's kisses soon melt her icy shell, but will they be enough to tempt her to take on this cowboy?

## #2925 RODEO REBEL

*Kingsland Ranch* • by Joanne Rock

With a successful bull rider in her bachelor auction, Lauryn Hamilton's horse rescue is sure to benefit. But rodeo star Gavin Kingsley has his devilish, bad boy gaze on *her*. The good girl. The one who's never ruled by reckless passion—until now...

## #2926 THE INHERITANCE TEST

by Anne Marsh

Movie star Declan Masterson needs to rehabilitate his playboy image fast to save his inheritance! Partnering with Jane Charlotte—the quintessential "plain jane"—for a charity yacht race is a genius first step. If only there wasn't a captivating woman underneath Jane's straightlaced exterior...

## #2927 BILLIONAIRE FAKE OUT

*The Image Project* • by Katherine Garbera

Paisley Campbell just learned her lover is a famous Hollywood A-lister... and she's expecting his baby! Sean O'Neill knows he's been living on borrowed time by keeping his identity secret. Can he convince her that everything they shared was not just a celebrity stunt?

## #2928 A GAME OF SECRETS

*The Eddington Heirs* • by Zuri Day

CEO Jake Eddington was charged with protecting his friend's beautiful sister from players and users. And he knows *he* should resist their chemistry too...but socialite Sasha McDowell is too captivating to ignore— even if their tryst ignites a scandal...

HDCNM1222

# HARLEQUIN
## PLUS

Announcing a **BRAND-NEW** multimedia subscription service for romance fans like you!

---

## Read, Watch and Play.

Experience the easiest way to get the romance content you crave.

Start your **FREE 7 DAY TRIAL** at
<u>www.harlequinplus.com/freetrial</u>.